CARIBBEAN FOLK TALES

STORIES FROM THE ISLANDS AND THE WINDRUSH GENERATION

WENDY SHEARER

First published 2022

The History Press
97 St George's Place, Cheltenham,
Gloucestershire, GL50 3QB
www.thehistorypress.co.uk

British Library Cataloguing in Publication Data.
A catalogue record for this book is available from the British Library.

ISBN 978 0 7509 9489 7

Typesetting and origination by The History Press.
Printed and bound in Great Britain by TJ Books Limited, Padstow, Cornwall.

Trees for Life

CONTENTS

FOREWORD

Whether it is the suspense aroused by watching an unsuspecting young male being lured away by the hypnotic powers of the legendary La Diablesse or the feeling of victory experienced with the discovery of the deceptive plan of 'the shapeshifting hog' who attempts to trick a young girl from a small village into marrying him, this collection of stories by Wendy Shearer will produce nostalgic moments of humour, reflection, and cultural connection for Caribbean readers across the globe. Caribbean Folk Tales: Stories from the islands and the Windrush Generation is a stimulating and thought-provoking creative collection which introduces readers to the rich, diverse culture and heritage of the Caribbean region.

The distinctive value of this collection lies in its ability to fuse together past and present worlds, unite different generations of readers, and celebrate the strong influence of Afro-Caribbean spirituality in the lives of Caribbean people. The collection offers an energized sense of continuity through the thematic placement of the different stories and through the sustained presence of orality established across each storytelling episode, showcasing the similarities which unite those from the Caribbean and the differences which cause each island to be unique. Through the invocation of a distinctly creolized set of voices and narrative style, Shearer artfully articulates stories involving legends, magical realism, songs, and proverbs which pull us back into a past lined with a rich Caribbean oral tradition, and place lessons at our fingertips, which we can readily access and appropriate to navigate our present-day realities. This Caribbean flavour is further enhanced by the presence of universal themes, such as the struggle of good versus evil, the plight of love, appearances versus reality, and the fight for freedom, which can be appreciated and enjoyed by readers across diverse cultures and ethnicities.

The ancestral practice of storytelling is presented throughout this collection as an act and process which restores, heals, and nurtures.

The collection balances fiction with non-fiction through both the morals embedded in the folktales in each chapter, and the presentation of autobiographical narratives from members of the Windrush generation through their personal and historical accounts of migration, memories of their homeland, and their participation in specific cultural practices. The folkloric frame used to characterize the tales in each chapter removes this genre of orality from the marginal places it tends to occupy in Western literary culture and emancipates the dominant historical narratives of some of the Caribbean mythical figures often defined in past European literary traditions as barbaric and soulless. Shearer's stories reposition these characters, so that their representation in this collection, now present them as heroes, heroines, or the figures who 'will disturb their neighbours', to use Bob Marley's description of referring to a personal act of activism which will emerge from an inner awakening and affect the entire community. The stories in this collection can be seen as significant artifacts which represent, affirm, and celebrate Caribbean identity and consciousness, especially in the face of racism, sexism, and issues of cultural prejudice in diasporic spaces. Additionally, the stories also subtly address patriarchal and stereotypical notions of identity and behaviour, subverting and challenging dominant ideologies that may have tainted some of the earlier accounts of these original, oral folktales.

Shearer's stories bring Caribbean legends and myths to life through the creative construction of different versions of these oral folktales adapted and retold in ways that provide valuable information about the histories, identities, and traditional practices of Caribbean people. By reshaping many of these well-known Caribbean myths, Shearer promotes the view that these tales are not to be characterized as mere superstition but instead to be hailed as coming through a storytelling pathway deeply embedded in the realm of the supernatural.

The collection fuses together an older, traditional folktale style with a more modern representation of voice and context where certain stories come to us through the rare use of the second person narrative voice which beckons the reader to be a part of the tale and to explore the magical worlds of the characters and settings present, establishing the call and response technique indicative of Afro-Caribbean culture.

Shearer creates an authentic experience for her readers through the detailed depictions of the many and varied Caribbean tales that have been such a significant part of the lives of Caribbean people over centuries, In the chapter Music and Songs, for example, we are softened by the presence of tragedy in stories like The Guitar Player, where a disheartened guitar player's ghost exacts revenge for the disregard he experiences at the hands of his community, while simultaneously we are moved when our sensibilities are awakened to the beauty of the musical rhythms and moments of dance.

Readers of this collection will be emboldened and inspired through stories of courage and bravery where the silenced or downtrodden right wrongs and disrupt acts of exploitation through skilful tactics and shrewd mindsets. Each of the stories presented in this collection sensitizes readers to the ways identity is deeply intertwined in the historical process of each Caribbean region and immediately connects readers with the full details of mythical characters, snippets of stories, and imagined worlds they are likely to have heard about through their parents, grandparents and/or great grandparents. Some of the fairy tales and legends remind us of virtues like patience, tolerance, and trust, while the cautionary tales encourage the celebration of a spirit of resilience and strength in the face of hardships and injustice.

The representation of Caribbean folklore and the unique presentation of Caribbean voices from the Windrush generation as part of the overall presentation of the stories in this collection, offer both young and old the opportunity to engage in a more personalized and sustained way with various aspects of Caribbean folklore and history. The stories here invite us to witness and participate in the enchanting and unforgettable worlds and encounters which have helped to shape Caribbean culture and experience. Open your minds and get ready to experience how something old can also become something new!

Dr Aisha T. Spencer, Phd
Senior Lecturer, Language and Literature Education,
University of the West Indies, Mona

ACKNOWLEDGEMENTS

A huge thank you to all the people from various Caribbean associations and friends who shared their personal stories and folklore with me, especially Rosamund Grant, Grace Hallworth, Winston Nzinga and Baden Prince.

Thanks also to Dr Philip Abraham, Caribbean collections expert within the Eccles Centre for American Studies at The British Library and Dr Aisha Spencer from The University of the West Indies.

Friends and family: Mum (Euline Stewart), Nan (Cleo Taitt), Uncle Maurice Taitt, Naomi Conroy-House, Gary Baron, Gary Bailey, Giles Abbott, Pippa Reid and especially my husband Matt Shearer, for their support, memories and introductions to their friends and family.

And thanks to illustrators Jenna Catton for the front cover and Mariko Aruga for the black and white illustrations throughout the book.

INTRODUCTION

Here you'll find a collection of folk tales and legends from a variety of Caribbean islands and mainland countries of Guyana and Suriname. The tales include stories of characters unique to each island, historical figures like Mary Seacole and legends of indigenous people – the Caribs and Tainos, who lived on the islands before European conquests. I've adapted these stories, and set them in the landscape of each island's history and culture where the wildlife and plants feature as important characters in their own right. Some stories are old and some are new, and most have been carried to the islands by enslaved Africans and blended with European and East Indian folklore. They've grown and transformed with each telling, reflecting cultural rituals that I've been introduced to by my Guyanese parents and grandparents.

The stories are usually told outside in the evenings on the islands, when old and young people gather together, always with rhythm and song. In this way, they continue the role of the African Griots who, for centuries, have been known to be the travelling storytellers and oral historians, preserving history and traditions.

I have arranged these folk tales into themes that reflect Caribbean culture, history and spirituality: Spirits & Shapeshifters; Music & Song; Tricksters; Love & Loss; and Caution & Justice. Many versions of these stories exist across different islands. You will meet the 'jumbie' spirit from Guyana, known as a 'duppy' in Jamaica, and the 'ol Higue' from Trinidad, known as the *soucouyant* in Haiti, who sheds her skin at night and transforms into a ball of fire, seeking out her victims. You'll also meet the renowned trickster Anansi, who began his journey with the Ashanti people of West Africa, considered to be the spirit of all knowledge and the keeper of the stories. In Caribbean folk tales he wilfully sneaks into situations, entering into the animal and human worlds where there are no boundaries; finding himself in trouble that he can often overcome.

Before each chapter I have included personal accounts from people who I have interviewed to capture their recollections of storytelling while growing up in the Caribbean, and their memories of leaving their island countries and arriving in the UK as a child. They migrated to England from these islands during the *Windrush* years and came to join their parents who were already in the UK working as nurses, bus drivers, engineers and construction workers. Many of them came to carve out a future for their families or to answer the request from the government to help rebuild Britain after the Second World War.

These oral histories are filled with bitter-sweet memories of leaving their Caribbean homes and embarking on a new life. Some of their childhood memories link to the themes of the folk tales where they were imagining smog-filled London crawling with spirits, loving the adventure of a new country, sad at leaving their old home or experiencing racial injustice in their new one. I spent many hours listening, documenting and travelling back in time with them. I feel incredibly privileged that they were happy to share their thoughts with me. The process itself of capturing their words was cathartic for those who had not shared these anecdotes before. Everyone recalled how oral storytelling was an integral part of their family life in the Caribbean.

The spirit and culture of black people are carried in the stories and songs, travelling across the islands and to the UK – wherever anyone goes. Despite the displacement of black people across countries, the stories are still passed down by generations, reflecting society and carrying wisdom.

Wherever we go, the stories go too.

Grace Hallworth, Trinidad

Grace Hallworth was a storyteller, librarian and author from Trinidad who published eighteen children's books. She appeared at many international festivals, on radio and on television, and served on a number of children's literature award panels. Her many books include Down by the River, *illustrated by Caroline Binch, which was a runner-up for the Kate Greenaway Medal in 1996. Grace had been the first Chair and long-standing patron of the Society for Storytelling. Sadly, she died in August 2021. She was a marvellous inspiration to children and adults who had the pleasure of hearing her vibrant voice bringing stories to life or reading her wonderful Caribbean folk tales and songs. When gathering stories for this book, I contacted Grace and she welcomed me into her home. We sipped ginger and apple juice, and in between tales, she shared memories of how she came to be in the UK.*

My storytelling journey began when I received a scholarship for Boys and Girls House in Canada. They empower young people and help develop their skills. I was 22 years old. It was in Canada that I found out, they were noted for storytelling. Eileen Colwell, who pioneered the children's library, and later founded the Association of Children's Librarians, was there too. They all fell in love with her because they had not seen anybody so involved and passionate about storytelling. I was lucky to end up at Boys and Girls House. I discovered the power of storytelling and stories there. I always enjoyed storytelling at home in Trinidad but there I found out what a powerful medium of communication it is.

Every Monday at Boys and Girls House, you had to present any book that you found interesting. I also told stories and they encouraged me to do that. That's how I began to take it seriously. In Trinidad, we told stories all the time, but no one really took me seriously. I was just 'Grace telling stories'. In Canada, they thought of it as having a serious power. Canada was the real start of my storytelling journey. During that time, I came over to Leeds in England to visit my friends and tell stories. It was my first visit to the UK. I liked it and enjoyed being here. I received a warm welcome from people and they wanted me to stay, but I was still in the middle of my scholarship and had to return to Trinidad for a short while.

Soon afterward, I was invited to Hertfordshire in England to develop children's literature and storytelling in libraries. They were very keen for me to come. Everything in the UK was moving in the direction that I wanted to go. I was also doing a lot of work with primary and secondary schools. I started as a Children's librarian and then I was promoted to Divisional Schools librarian. Soon my work expanded to other places, including general adult libraries and hospitals. Once they heard that I was telling stories, they wanted me too. The momentum was building.

Soon after that, Ben Haggarty and I got together and we formed a society for storytelling. We were extremely keen to do this and knew that we needed to invite storytellers from other places, festivals, theatres, and all kinds of events. This was a new chapter in my storytelling journey. You might say that I was fortunate in that everything worked in my favour.

Euline Stewart, Guyana

Education and Mediation Consultant

I came to England in 1964 with two of my younger brothers. I was 12 years old and we flew on the British Overseas Airways Corporation flight, better known as BOAC. Our neighbour was also travelling to England on the same flight with her two daughters and she had agreed to be the guardian for my youngest brother, who was 4 years old at the time.

We never came to England together as a family. No families did at that time. My dad came first, arriving in 1962, and then once he had managed to find a decently sized house for us, he sent for my mum, who came in

1963. The rest of us remained living in Guyana with our grandparents, while my parents were working in England. Before emigrating to London, we had all lived together as a family in one big house in West Ruimveldt Housing Scheme and so it didn't feel unusual when our parents left to travel and live abroad because we were still with my grandparents. However, we were separated as a family for a total of two years.

I was so excited about coming to England, because as children we were told the streets were paved with gold and that there was no mud! I was expecting it to be so sunny and clean, just like it was in Guyana. I arrived on 31 October 1964 (late into the evening) and it was extremely cold, dark, foggy and snowing. I remember the street lamps had a yellow glow and looked very dim, which made me feel very unhappy. This was the first time I had seen snow. The fog was so intense that I could hardly see anything in front of me. We'd never seen that before and we definitely didn't see any gold on the streets! London seemed very weird to me as a child. When we were walking on the pavement, we'd see people walking out of their basement house in the midst of the fog as if they were rising like jumbies (ghosts) from the street. I thought this was a bizarre sight to see at the time and quickly hastened my steps and walked as fast as I could.

After a few days of living in London, I wanted to go back to Guyana, because the weather was very cold and I wasn't used to it. We had to wear gloves (or mittens) on our hands and boots on our feet. Sometimes you couldn't feel your toes! Your nose and ears would get extremely cold and I began to suffer from nosebleeds a lot! My father told me that 'I'll get used to the weather'.

Just before I left Guyana, I had passed my 11+ to go to Bishop's Girls' High School. This was the only top girls' school in Georgetown and I was sad that I wasn't able to join my friends to attend the school because I was coming to England to join my parents instead. We lived in south London and my dad enrolled me at Westwood Girls' High School. The teachers immediately placed me in the bottom sets, because they assumed that as I had not been educated in England that I must be backward (a label I later discovered was given to West Indian children as being educationally subnormal). The standard of teaching in Guyana was extremely high when I was living there. My dad insisted that I be tested on the first day of school and I was tested vigorously in what they termed spoken English and maths, which included algebra, fractions, logarithms, measuring various types of angles, etc. I sailed through the tests and was placed in the middle B sets for maths and English. The headteacher was amazed that I had such knowledge in mathematics for my age. After six months, I was moved mid-year up to the 'A' stream and remained there until what we now call Year 11. I was the first and only black student in that top set at school.

I enjoyed school and had no problems. My brothers were at the local boys' school. I remember that the joy of living in London was not hearing the singing sound of mosquitoes or even being bitten by them! They were and still are Guyana's most common flying insect. I hated them, because when they bit you, the typical reactions to the bite are itching and swelling, which can cause a serious illness such as malaria. Education has remained a really important part of my life. After achieving my M.A. in Education, I have been a mentor for young black and ethnic minority youths, an inclusion officer to prevent exclusions in primary schools and now I am an education and mediation consultant, helping people to resolve conflicts when communication links have broken down.

I did miss gathering together as a family to hear stories when we were in Guyana. Storytelling and folk music was a part of our lives in Guyana. Our grandmother would tell us stories of jumbies and shapeshifters to frighten us as a child at night and stories of Anansi the wise trickster. If any of us told a fib, my gran would say, that's 'nancy story you telling me'.

Spirits & Shapeshifters

Many Caribbean folk tales are filled with ghosts and magical creatures, reflecting a history of African spirituality and the afterlife. The stories share warnings or moral teachings about life on the islands and these are my versions of a few familiar tales that are told in different ways throughout the islands. Some people believe these events happened or may have partially happened. I'll let you decide.

La Diablesse

Martinique

Long, long ago, on the Caribbean island of Martinique, the French still ruled and Creole was the spoken word. It emerged from the rich medley of French and African languages, created by the enslaved Africans. On this picturesque island, the mountains would erupt and lava would flow freely into valleys, burying everything in its wake. Hurricanes would rampage through villages, wiping out factories and ripping up trees. With all of these violent horrors lurking among the villagers, it might surprise you to know who they feared most. La Diablesse.

Some people said she was a she-devil. A jumbie with a disfigured foot that resembles a hoof. Others said that she was a witch, roaming the highways alone, waiting to cast her vengeful spells on unsuspecting men. Everyone said to watch out, beware and be on your guard for strangers in your village.

The story goes that on one typically blazing hot day, people were stretched out on their verandas, sighing in the shade. Watching nothing. Imagine a day so hot that even the air is languid, where each breath you take is a slow, dragging movement. Two young men, Kabenla and Ekoux, were sitting outside of their boarding house. They'd stopped for lunch after working all morning at the sugar factory and sat staring into the distance, watching nothing in particular. The sweet scent of mango hung in the air from trees dotted around the houses. Goats ambled across the paths, nibbling at leaves and long grass.

'Kabenla, you notice how quiet it is today?' Ekoux nudged his friend. Even though it was the middle of the day, with sunlight exposing every living thing, Ekoux felt a darkness creeping up around them. He glanced around. He had a sense that something was not quite right. Houses seemed hushed into silence with their shutters closed up. Trees appeared monstrous behind him, terror swaying with each branch.

'Kabenla, did you hear me?' Ekoux asked his friend again.

'Ease me Ekoux, can't you see I'm busy?'

Ekoux followed Kabenla's gaze. Seemingly out of nowhere in the brilliant light of day, a tall, slender woman was striding through the village. Her pace was at odds with the sluggish heat of the day. Her long arms swayed back and forth, driving her body forward. Her colourful clothes draped unnaturally around her body, stiff and lifeless. She wore a short-sleeved blouse and a long madras skirt that fell rigid to the ground. Glimpses of her white ruffled petticoat could be seen as she glided along. Her face was partially hidden by a wide-brimmed straw hat. She was dark, serene, and heading their way.

'Look how her hips are swaying. You see her eyes?' Kabenla said, in a daze. It's true, she did have the most exquisite-looking eyes but they were not welcoming. They were cold and glassy. Set deep into her face like obsidian rock. She went past the boarding house.

'*Bonjou mesye*, hello sir,' she nodded firmly, without stopping.

'*Bonjou madanm*, hello madam,' Kabenla replied. He jumped up from his seat and quickly fell into step with her.

'Eh, eh, you look as sweet as molasses,' he said with a wide grin. She did not reply or even look at him.

And so it begins again. She sighed to herself. She was used to getting unwanted attention from men. At first, she felt flattered by it, as she travelled from village to village, seeking a new home after the loss of her own. Men would compliment her, offer her work on their land, even appear to befriend her. She had been naive but now she could exact her revenge. She carried on striding while Kabenla carried on talking.

'I've never seen you here before. *Ki kote ou soti*? Where are you from?'

'Affairs of the chicken are not affairs of the goat,' she replied, keeping her dark eyes facing straight ahead. She thought Kabenla was the same as all the other men before him. The ones who would look right through her clothes to her dark naked skin. The ones who would undress her in their mind as they followed her every move.

'Why so serious?' Kabenla wanted to know.

'I'm in mourning. I died long ago.' Perhaps she was just joking or trying to shock. Either way, Kabenla took no notice.

'Would you like some company?' he offered, puffing up his chest.

She stopped and stared at him for the first time. 'Before climbing up a tree, make sure you can climb down.' Her tone was not unfriendly and yet not quite inviting. Under the brim of her hat, he saw his reflection in her eyes. Those dark eyes.

'I'm walking up high, where the cinnamon spices grow and the rainfall is plenty,' her voice seemed to soar right into the mountains when she spoke. Kabenla knew that she was heading far away from his village. He'd never make it back in time for his afternoon shift at the factory. He turned back to look at his friend. Ekoux was shaking his head and waving his arms, signalling for Kabenla to return. For some reason unknown to him, Kabenla felt compelled to go with this woman. He was captivated by her. Instead of heading back to his friend and the boarding house, he followed her right out of the village.

They walked along the road from Balata, a path that twisted and turned with the barks of the trees. Iguanas were lazing across the branches and manicous sniffed the grass with their long snouts. No other living person was around. They were completely alone. She marched on and kept a steady pace, without looking back. Kabenla struggled to keep up with her.

Sweat dripped from his brow and his white shirt clung to his chest. He was used to this moist heat but it seemed as if they had been walking for hours. He tried again to spark up conversation.

'*Kijan ou rele*? What is your name?'

'*Fè yon devine*. Guess,' she said. Her dimples deepened, barely concealing a smile.

'Marie?

'No.'

'Isabelle?'

'No.'

'Isaora?'

'You'll never guess.'

'I. Give. Up.' Kabenla was out of breath. The air felt paper thin. They were high up in the mountains now and the path was steeper. Even though he was tired, he wanted to climb with her forever. She was walking faster, with no trace of tiredness or discomfort. Her long, brightly coloured skirt dragged over the rocks. She was slightly ahead of him, just out of sight. He followed the sound of her ruffled petticoat. The smell of sweet cinnamon hung from the leaves. They must be close, he thought, feeling a rush of dizzying excitement. He did not notice the darkness creeping in all around them.

Earlier that afternoon, Ekoux had returned to work at the factory and was disappointed that Kabenla had left him to it.

'I can't believe he's run off to chase a bit of skirt,' he grumbled to his friends. They laughed, accusing him of being jealous. After all, if a tall, striking woman spoke to them, who would not follow her? They worked until early evening, once the sun had been swallowed up by the darkness.

Ekoux headed home, wondering what tall tales his friend would conjure up for his absence. I bet he will say she kept him captive and wouldn't let him go. He laughed to himself, preparing to listen to all kinds of outlandish stories of how Kabenla had spent his afternoon while the rest of them were working hard.

Back at the boarding house, he expected to see his friend sitting with his feet up on the veranda, sipping from a bottle of beer, ready to boast about his afternoon. But as Ekoux approached the steps, there was no sign of him sitting outside. The trees swayed gently, whispering all around him. The air felt lighter than it had today. Gone was the peculiar feeling of terror that he'd felt earlier. Perhaps Kabenla was hiding in his room.

Ekoux knocked on his door.

'Hey man, what are you playing at? Where have you been?'

He waited for a reply or some movement from inside but heard no answer. He pushed open the door and saw that the room was empty. Perhaps Kabenla was helping to prepare dinner.

He heard the sound of bowls being scraped and lids being placed onto clay pots. The smell of conch stew with onions and spices grabbed him. He realised he was hungry and needed to eat. He entered the kitchen and his grumbling changed to worrying when there was still no sign of Kabenla. They never missed a meal together. He ate quickly and decided to ask around. No one seemed worried.

'He's a grown man. What are you worrying about?' was the most common response he received. Fear crept over Ekoux as it was not like his friend to disappear for this long. He strolled outside and wandered around asking anyone he saw if they knew where he had gone.

'*Bonswa*. Good evening. Have you seen my friend Kabenla? About this tall, wearing a white shirt like mine.' He gesticulated wildly to neighbours in the village.

'He was with a tall, elegant woman. A stranger. He walked off with her at lunchtime,' explained Ekoux. No one took any notice except for one elderly man who had been liming on the side of the road for most of the afternoon. He shook his head solemnly and asked Ekoux, 'Was this woman quite tall and walking fast?'

'Yes. And she had a large straw hat. Did you see them?' he asked again.

'No.' He replied. Ekoux turned to leave.

'It sounds to me like La Diablesse,' he tutted loudly, still shaking his head. Ekoux had run out of patience and was about to curse the man.

'Listen to me. La Diablesse is a she-devil who haunts these mountain roads. If your friend left with her you might never see him again.' Ekoux had heard these tales before but didn't want to believe them. They were stories told to frighten and keep you from trusting strangers.

'There's no way a jumbie spirit showed up in broad daylight!' yelled Ekoux.

The old man shook his head again. 'Don't be so sure, young man. Some terrors appear right beside us in the day.' He shuffled off and left Ekoux wondering if there was any truth to these stories.

Up in the mountains, the sun had disappeared beneath the trees long ago, allowing the darkness to leap out. One minute, Kabenla was scrambling along a rocky path, following the stranger's shapely silhouette, and then suddenly he was plunged into blackness.

'Where are you? I can't see you,' he cried out. He wasn't usually a fearful man but he knew it was dangerous to be stumbling around at night. The night critters grew louder and he felt them close. She had not slowed down. She kept moving. He couldn't understand how she was able to navigate so deftly, when he couldn't even see his own hands in front of his face. He reached out for her and lost his balance.

She smiled in the darkness, surprised that he'd kept up with her for so long. She used to wait until they pounced. When their appetite overcame their senses. She could see it in their eyes. Now, she didn't wait. She pounced first.

'*Swiv vwa mwen!* Follow my voice!' She cried out.

In the darkness, he heard her chant. The words rose up from her belly and clawed their way out of her throat. He couldn't understand them but he felt their power. Her voice thundered into the night sky.

Akwaaba
Akwaaba
Me din de
Ɔbonsam

Akwaaba
Akwaaba
Me din de
Ɔbonsam

As she chanted, a violent gust of wind swirled around them. The shadows sank their teeth into his bones.

'Are you scared?' her voice was mocking. A chill crept up his spine. He suddenly felt like a spell was broken. He no longer found her captivating. He thought she was terrifying.

'Take my hand.' She reached out and touched him. Her hand felt like stone, cold and bloodless.

'*Vini*. Come.' She ordered. Reluctantly, he followed her. She turned to look at him, half lit by the moon. He saw a wretched expression on her face. Everything was contorted. Her eyes flared with hell's fury, her mouth gnarled and twisted, like a tiger with its prey. He shrieked and shrank back further, moving away from her towards the cliff edge. His feet slipped in the dirt. He tried to lurch forward but he lost his grip and fell swiftly over the edge.

An empty cry came from his lips as he hit the rocks 2,000ft below. No one heard him except La Diablesse. There in the moonlight, you could see the imprint of her hoof mark in the dirt as she shuffled away.

The Shapeshifting Hog

Trinidad

There once lived a young girl in a small village, on the picturesque island of Trinidad. The last island on that southern curve floating in the Caribbean sea. Clara was her name and she was causing tongues to wag and fingers to point. All because she refused to marry any of the local boys who came knocking at the farmhouse, where she lived with her parents and grandmother. You see,

Clara was not only striking with dark waves of hair and brick-red skin. She was also extremely clever like her mother and mother's mother, with bright, knowing eyes that carried generations of wisdom. She was in no rush to marry just anyone. Now, these were the days when it was respectful to ask a father's permission to marry his daughter. Suiters would often try their luck thinking, 'Maybe I have a chance with Clara today?'

They'd get dressed up in their Sunday best. Shoes polished with vaseline, shirt freshly washed and afro cropped low. Then they'd walk boldly across her father's land. They'd reach the wooden staircase leading to Clara's verandah and slowly climb, practising their greetings.

Step one, 'Howdy Clara, you're looking fine today.'

Step two, 'Here, I've picked some sour-sweet tamarind for you.'

Step three, 'Will you sit on the verandah with me?'

By the time they'd reached the fourth step, Clara would have made up her mind. She'd watch from an upstairs window, thinking:

He too mauger.
He too bol' face.
He too cock eye.

You can imagine how this went down with the villagers. Tongues would wag and fingers would point. You could hear mothers whispering when buying saltfish in the market square: 'That Clara always skin-up she nose.' While listening to the pastor in church on Sundays: 'You see her? She refused to see my boy Robert.' While sipping soursop punch at Carnival time: 'Is that Clara here? Cockroach has no right at a fowl party.'

And so it went on. Until one fine day, a tall, dark, handsome stranger by the name of Clayton floated into their village on the Caribbean breeze. Dressed from head to toe in shades of ocean blue and a straw hat, the colour of sunshine, he charmed everyone including Clara with his sweet mouth, as we say.

Clayton made it all the way up the front steps and to Sunday lunch. Afterward, they'd sit outside on the veranda, only inches apart on an easy chair. Joined only by the chorus of the frogs and crickets, they'd rock back and forth together. He'd look deep into her eyes.

'Oh Clara, the stars are surely dimmed tonight without you there to shine.' Oh yes, he really said that. He entertained her with calypso songs carrying news from near and far. Every day, he turned up to their home, laden with provisions for her family, singing:

> I have sweet potato, cassava too
> Yellow plantain that's good for you
> Come, leh we eat some.

His voice rang out across the field, his arms filled with sweet potatoes, yams, cassava and plantains. Her family loved him and so did she. Before you could say 'jack robin', he popped the question. 'Can I marry your daughter?' Her father was pleased, her mother was pleased and her grandmother was not displeased. The local boys were furious. They had been spurned for this flashy stranger who was charming all the girls and their elders with his sweet songs and sweet potatoes. Once again, tongues would wag and fingers would point.

'Where did he spring from? Where does he get all that food from?' These questions plagued Clara, too. She noticed that he always seemed to be in a hurry to leave her just before the sunset. If you have been to the Caribbean, you will know that the sun never sets slowly. It drops suddenly. Darkness comes thick and fast. Clayton would kiss Clara on her cheek, throw on his suit jacket, and hustle out of her home, just before the fireflies could be seen lighting up the grass. He'd make his way deep into the forest. Past the cocoa field and sweet-smelling mango groves. He'd head to a clearing surrounded by silk cotton trees. Their tall slender trunks, like giant beanstalks are said to be keepers of spirits and secrets. In that clearing, away from watchful eyes and wagging tongues, Clayton began to chant:

> Sha-ling. My name is Clayton
> Sha-ling. I come for Clara.

Dancing and waving his arms furiously as he sang, with each line he stripped off a piece of his clothing:

Sha-ling.

He took off his jacket.

My name is Clayton.

He ripped off his shirt.

Sha-ling.

He kicked off his shoes.

I come for Clara.

He pulled down his trousers.

He bent over onto all fours as his naked body began to change shape. His legs became short with trotters at the end. His nose stretched into a long snout. His skin thickened with dark, coarse bristles. Clayton had transformed into a snorting, grunting hog. He shuffled into the undergrowth digging up sweet potatoes and yams that rose from the earth with his chant. Before the sun rose, Clayton growled out the words to his chant:

Sha-ling. My name is Clayton.
Sha-ling. I come for Clara.

His body began to shift back into its human form. His long snout shortened into a nose, his thick bristles disappeared, his stumpy trotters grew back into long, shapely legs. He put back on his clothes and hurried out of the forest, back into the village, carrying an armful of provisions he'd dug up from the earth.

Imagine that? What a sight and no one was there to witness it. Except Clara was having a few doubts about this handsome young stranger who disappeared at the onset of darkness. 'Where did he go? Did he have another girlfriend?' What would you think? What would you do? She decided to follow him and find out for herself.

One night, after they all shared a hearty meal of curry duck with roti, Clara stood at the front door, watching Clayton hurry away into the twilight. That shadowy part of the day that belongs neither to darkness nor light. She tiptoed down their wooden staircase, ran through the cocoa field, and slipped into the forest behind Clayton. She watched and waited in the bushes as he entered the clearing of silk cotton trees. Suddenly Clayton's voice soared high above the canopy of leaves:

Sha-ling. My name is Clayton.
Sha-ling. I come for Clara.

Clara saw his limbs waving furiously as he danced. Her eyes widened with terror as he threw off his clothes one by one and shapeshifted into a grunting hog, with trotters and a long snout. Her legs buckled as the ground stirred and provisions of root vegetables rose up from the soil. She hurried back home to tell her father what she had seen. He was sceptical to say the least. Well, wouldn't you be if your daughter announced that your future son-in-law was really a shapeshifting hog?

'Clara, what kind of nonsense is this? He rocked back and forth on the verandah chair, pipe in hand, smoke swirling into the starlit sky. 'Too late to find fault with this man. Your wedding will take place in two days' time and that is that.'

Clara's fate was sealed. Her father liked Clayton. He liked the food that he brought and the songs that he sang.

Her grandmother and mother were soaking beans overnight in the kitchen. They listened in silence to Clara's tale.

'Grandmother what shall I do? Father won't send him away.'

Her soft brown face, creased with years gone by, came close to her granddaughter's ear.

'Clara, every hog has his market day,' she whispered.

'Time to take matters into your own hands,' sighed her mother.

With the help of her mother and grandmother, Clara gathered a long piece of black cloth and attached animal parts to it. Chicken feet, pigtails, cow feet, and fish heads dangled freely from the material. They waited for Clayton to leave their home as usual and then all three women followed him. Under the cloak of darkness, they blended into the forest. It wasn't long before Clayton was waving his arms furiously and chanting. He removed his clothes and his voice pierced through the night once more:

> Sha-ling sha-ling. My name is Clayton.
> Sha-ling sha-ling. I come for Clara.

Just before his human form peeled away, Clayton saw a glow in the distance. Flickers of orange and yellow shifted between the trees. Mesmerised, he walked towards the bright glow. Just past the silk cotton trees he saw a beast dancing wildly in front of a fire. It towered above the flames, at least the height of two men. Cow feet, chicken feet, fish heads clung to its large body. Six arms stretched out, pounding long spears into the ground:

> Sha-ling sha-ling. My name is Clara
> Sha-ling sha-ling. I come for Clayton's head.
> Sha-ling sha-ling. My name is Clara.
> Sha-ling sha-ling. I come for Clayton's feet.

Without waiting to hear anything else, Clayton turned and ran. He didn't even stop to pick up his shirt. He darted out of the forest and left the village. Clara removed the dark cloak of hanging animal parts and threw down the wild canes, which looked like spears. She climbed down off the shoulders of her mother, who climbed down off the shoulders of her grandmother.

The three women sat around the fire, laughing at how they'd chased a shapeshifting hog right out of their lives.

THE OLD HIGUE

Trinidad

Let me tell you a story that took place many years ago in the tiny village of Toco on the island of Trinidad. This village is far in the north, right at the point where the Atlantic Ocean meets the Caribbean Sea. Back then, there were no roads leading to this village from the mainland. It could only be reached by boat. Toco was so remote and quiet in the mountains. Anything could happen. And almost anything did.

In this village, surrounded by cacao trees and coffee plants, there was an old woman. Ma Coo was her name. She lived on the outskirts of the village, just far enough not to be bothered by anyone unless they wanted her help. You see, Ma Coo was known as an *obeah* woman. A woman who practised witchcraft. *Obeah* is a sorcery that had been secretly kept alive by enslaved Africans. They were stripped of their language and religion. They were even prohibited from using drums to communicate. But they were allowed to wear amulets filled with herbs around their necks and to mix potions for medicine. This is how the *obeah* lived on.

Ma Coo knew these ways of old. She had lived so long, no one knew of a time when she was not there. Her long wavy hair was crystal white with age. Yet her dark skin remained smooth without lines, as if untouched by time. Men and women would visit Ma Coo if they had a problem they needed help with. Perhaps to bring the new harvest in. Or a boss who won't give you a raise. A man who you suspect has slept with your wife. Someone you want to fall in love with you.

She would cast spells and grant all their desires for a fee. Her only rule was, 'Don't cross me and I won't cross you.'

Usually, people were happy with the results of these spells, but there was one man who was not. Cyrus Evans. He owned a thriving coffee plantation and came to Ma Coo one day for a spell of abundance.

'I want to be the biggest supplier of coffee in the country,' he whispered when they met one night. 'I want everyone to know my name.' She gave him a sachet of black salt made from the ashes of incense.

'Sprinkle this around your office,' she advised. She waited until sunlight drew its last breath to begin her spell and then she welcomed the darkness in. With candles lit around her kitchen, Ma Coo ground cinnamon bark with bitter herbs and muttered her incantation. Her hands danced over the dimly lit flames and her body swayed to the rhythm of her words until the spell was cast.

Who knows what Cyrus Evans was expecting to happen but he decided that Ma Coo was fake. He refused to pay. Not only did he refuse to pay but he started bad-mouthing her to neighbours. The foul stench of rumour spread around Toco village, dragging Ma Coo's reputation with it. She was called a 'fake' and a 'trickster' and soon five others refused to pay for her help.

Some of you may already be aware of the silent contract you enter into with a witch. Secrecy is paramount. Witches know your deepest fears and hidden weaknesses. And you know of their abilities. So here was Ma Coo, being talked about behind her back and ridiculed right to her face. Perhaps they felt emboldened by Cyrus Evans. Or maybe they simply forgot her one rule. Do you remember? 'Don't cross me and I won't cross you.'

Now her rule had been broken. It was only a matter of time before Ma Coo would get her revenge. Villagers today remember it well. They would have been young when they heard what happened but the memory of it is indelibly printed on their minds.

It began on a night filled with vivid terror when ghastly death ripped its claws through the village. Cyrus went to sleep that night when the moon was high and the air was still. His bedroom window had been left open a crack. Sleeping deeply, he did not see a ball of flames floating across the fields, littered with slender trees of cacao pods, hanging down like crimson leaves. He was unaware of the fire darting through the tamarind trees. It swiftly made its way through his open window and silently shapeshifted into an old woman. She turned her monstrous gaze towards his body, bit his neck, and sucked the life right out of him. There were five other

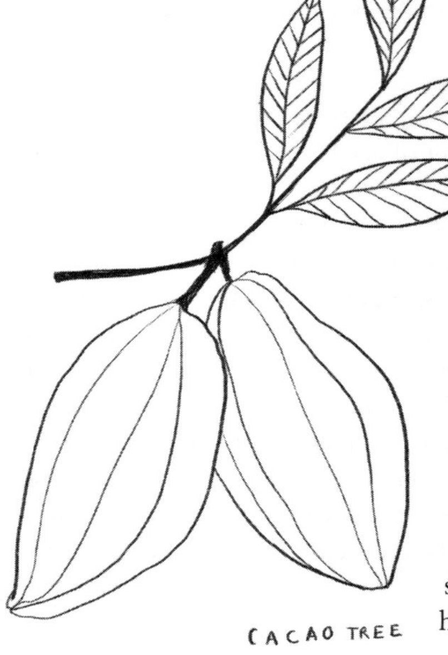

deaths that week, where people's blood had been drained from their bodies. They were all found the following morning, their flesh hanging from their bones, shrivelled with two bite marks on each of their necks.

One unexpected death may arouse curiosity but six violent deaths caused great suspicion, which fell squarely at the feet of old Ma Coo.

'I know it was her. That woman is wicked.'

'She worked her *obeah* on them.'

These were the conversations taking place in the fish market and on the stoops at night. It did not go unnoticed that the people who died were the ones who bad-mouthed Ma Coo the most. Cyrus' wife went to visit one of the elders in their village, a man named old man Wilkie. She was worried that more deaths might happen and asked him for his advice. She found him on his front verandah, rocking back and forth on his chair. There was little going on in the village that old man Wilkie didn't know about. He listened in silence, while she told of Cyrus refusing to pay Ma Coo.

'I saw a ball of fire rising above my house,' he said gravely. I've not seen that for a very long time.'

'What does it mean?' she asked. He explained that there was an 'old Higue' in their village. Some call her a *soucouyant*. A shapeshifter who removes her skin at night and transforms into a flaming ball of fire looking for her victims. Cyrus' wife had heard the horror stories but did not want to believe it.

'First', said old man Wilkie. 'You need to gather white chalk, pepper and a pile of rice to protect yourselves and defeat it.' He beckoned her to come closer as he whispered how to capture the old Higue.

She gathered her courage and shared old man Wilkie's advice with a few friends. Together they closed up windows and sealed up locks around the village. They placed a pile of rice grains on the path where four roads meet, leading to Ma Coo's house. They waited until nightfall and the gentle hum of nocturnal critters before hiding in the bushes near Ma Coo's house.

Late into the night, when the duppies walk freely and the shapeshifters roam, Ma Coo transformed into the old Higue. She slowly peeled off her skin and placed it carefully into a calabash under her bed for when she returned. Her fleshless form, shapeshifted into a flaming ball of fire, which flew out of her open window and into the waiting night.

She found her neighbours' windows firmly closed and locks sealed up. Everyone was safely protected with circles of white chalk around their homes. The old Higue flew to the centre of the village and came across the pile of rice on the path where four roads meet. Compelled by an ancient curse to stop and count each grain, the old Higue had no choice but to pick up the rice and begin her slow count.

Cyrus's wife and her friends had broken into Ma Coo's house in search of her skin. They found it in the calabash under her bed.

'This is proof that she really is an old Higue,' they agreed and sprinkled pepper all over it just as old man Wilkie had advised.

'If she returns before sunrise can vaporise her, she will never be able to climb back into her skin now,' they continued. They need not have worried, for the sun rose high in the east and glared with all its might directly at the old Higue, who was still counting grains of rice. She screamed out in anguish as the sunlight melted her form, reducing her to a pile of ashes on the path.

To this very day, no one walks on the spot where the four roads meet, for fear of invoking the spirit of the old Higue in Toco village.

All That Glitters

Guyana

Not that long ago, there was a man who had been searching for 'the one'. Someone he could share his life and wealth with. Lionel was his name and he was tall and broad like the Mora tree, with shoulders stretching towards the sky. His skin was the deepest shade of midnight. His search had led him through villages, towns, countries, and even across continents. He'd seen many wonders and collected many exquisite garments and treasures.

His search took him to the northern tip of Guyana, with its dense rainforests and deep gold mines. He sailed across the wine-dark Essequibo river until he reached the larger of the West Demerara islands.

Here, he happened upon a small village known as Free and Easy. No one really knows how it came to have that name. I like to think it's because the people there are so laid back and welcoming. Free and Easy is a long walk from the mainland. With only the blistering heat for company, Lionel slung his blue, silk suit jacket over his shoulder, unbuttoned his crisp white shirt and strolled along the dirt track, carrying two leather cases from Marrakesh in each hand. People shuffled past, cows raised their sleepy heads and eyed up this stranger in their land. As with any small village, news of his arrival spread fast, blowing in on the sea breeze with faint smells of lime trees and fresh coconut.

'You see that tall, dark-skinned man? Did you catch his gold bracelet? His leather cases?' Lionel strolled along and smiled at the ladies selling shave ice on Durum road. He nodded at the men, liming outside of the rum shop, sipping their Banks beer. He soon came to a wooden house on giant stilts. It was the only boarding house in the village. It was painted a flamboyant blue, with a sign hanging from the porch that read 'Alana's Place'. Singing was coming from within:

> Our dinner will soon be done done done,
> I have sweet potatoes with callaloo
> Frying fish and ochroes too
> Our dinner will soon be done done done.

I don't know if it was the voice that captivated him or the smell of frying fish and spices, but Lionel drifted up those steps and into the house. He followed the singing, which took him to the kitchen where Alana was. He saw her halo of thick black hair, hips swinging from side to side and hands stirring and turning at the stove. Alana looked up and drank in his gaze.

'And what breeze did you blow in on?' Her voice was music to his ears. She smiled. Without missing a soca beat, she carried right on singing.

From that moment on they were inseparable. The next day, she showed him around the village.

'Here is the rum shop run by my cousin Leicester. Here is the post office that receives post once a month from the mainland. This is the cassava farm.' Her face lit up, like morning sunrise when she spoke. Villagers shook their heads and whispered, 'What a fuss she is making over this stranger.'

The next night Lionel told her stories of his travels. And what a storyteller he was!

'Let me tell you about the time I chased away the Lagahoo.' For those of you who may not know, the Lagahoo is what some may call a werewolf. Neighbours gathered around him, sharing tales like they did every night under the moon's bright eye.

'Come close. Let me tell you how my friend met his death, at the hands of La Diablesse.' For those of you who may not know, some say La Diablesse is a 'she-devil'.

The days and nights went on like that, with Alana cooking and singing for him and Lionel dazzling her with his stories. Soon he proposed and she accepted. But her family was not so keen.

'What do you know about him?' asked her father.

'He's just showing off himself,' said her brother

'Give the local boys a chance nuh,' said her sister.

'All that glitters is not gold,' said her mother.

Cast your mind back to when you were young and deliriously in love. Would you have heeded a warning from your family? They married under the scarlet flame tree in the courtyard of the village church. Without so much as a second glance, they set off for Lionel's home, across the Caribbean Sea.

When they arrived in Trinidad, Lionel explained, 'I need to return something I borrowed from a friend.' He gave back his beautiful leather-bound cases from Marrakesh. Alana thought nothing of it. They continued to sail on through Grenada and when they arrived he said the same thing, 'I need to return something I borrowed from a friend.' He gave back his exquisite, blue silk suit, from Sukhumvit road in Bangkok. Alana thought, 'That's a shame, he looked so smart and attractive in that.'

When they stopped off in St Vincent, she marvelled at its white sandy beaches and coconut palm trees towering above them. They feasted on pumpkin soup, breadfruit and the legendary fried jackfish. In the midst of their honeymoon bliss, Lionel met a friend and gave back his gold bracelet.

Alana was growing deeply suspicious now and asked, 'Is there anything you own?'

But this carried on at each island. When they stopped off in Barbados, that slice of paradise that you can tour around in a day, they dined on flying fish and he gave back his crisp white shirt.

In St Lucia, he gave back his gold tooth.

In Dominica he gave back his gold watch and chain.

In Montserrat, the Pompeii of the Caribbean, known for its dramatic volcanoes, he gave back his gold wedding ring.

In Antigua, he gave back his hairpiece.

In Puerto Rico, he gave back his legs.

In Haiti, he pulled out his eyes.

Fear crept over Alana's face like a spider in the night.

'Oh lord', she cried. 'I married a jumbie.' She was right. Lionel was a demon spirit who had finally revealed his true self!. Alone on the island of Hispaniola between the Caribbean Sea and the north Atlantic Ocean, her mother's words came back to haunt her: 'All that glitters is not gold.'

The Curse of Mama D'leau

Trinidad

It is well known on the tropical islands that the water people are the creatures who dwell in the murky rivers and black creeks. They are the ones who protect the fishes and waters that flow through dense forests and down steep mountainsides teeming with tree ferns. These creatures are the fairymaids and mermaids whose lives and powers are inextricably linked to the creatures of the forest. Pollute the waters, hunt down or harm the animals and you'll find yourselves at the mercy of Mama D'leau. This is the story of one man who found out the hard way.

Tomas of Mayo village was a young man with ambitions beyond his 20 years of age. He'd grown up hearing stories about the mer-folk lore on the island of Trinidad. He'd been told about Mama D'leau, whose name means 'Water Mother'. Known as the fierce protector of the rivers, she is half woman, half sea serpent and the islanders believed she would punish anyone who polluted the waters or harmed the fish.

It is said that Mama D'leau is the lover of Papa Bois, the man with goat horns and hooves who protects the forest and its animals. Together they rule over the wild creatures that blend between our world and theirs, the realm where spirits and magic coexist.

Despite these beliefs, which had flourished from the myths carried to the islands by enslaved Africans generations before, Tomas paid no attention to the warnings. He had made up his mind that his fortune could be made by hunting and trapping the fish and forest animals. He knew that money could be made from those eager to buy.

'I'm going to get rich real quick,' Tomas would say to his friends as they hung out down by the river. 'There's plenty of fish in these rivers and deer to hunt in the forest.' He could see an abundance of kingfisher birds and ducklings scurrying around. There were ripples of water made from all the fishes circling down below and he began to plan how he'd capture as much wildlife as possible and sell it in the villages.

His father and grandfather were seamen, taking their vessels out to sea late at night, returning with wild fish and equally wild stories of creatures haunting the seas. They told Tomas that his ambitions were reckless and tried to warn him that the seamen fished further out at sea for a reason. 'You know these rivers are protected by Mama D'leau?' Grandfather, who was sipping rum on his veranda one night, leaned in to Tomas and said in hushed tones. 'You crave all, and get none at all my boy.'

But Tomas was of a new generation. He had courage and stubbornness jutting from his young jaw. 'Grandfather, I don't believe in any of that old-time foolishness,' he replied. 'I'm a man of vision. I make my own destiny.'

Later that night when the moon lit up the waters with its soft glow, Tomas laid his fishing traps in the river. He waded in and dropped his net filled with bait and tied the line to a huge rock on the edge of the river bank. No one on land saw him come or

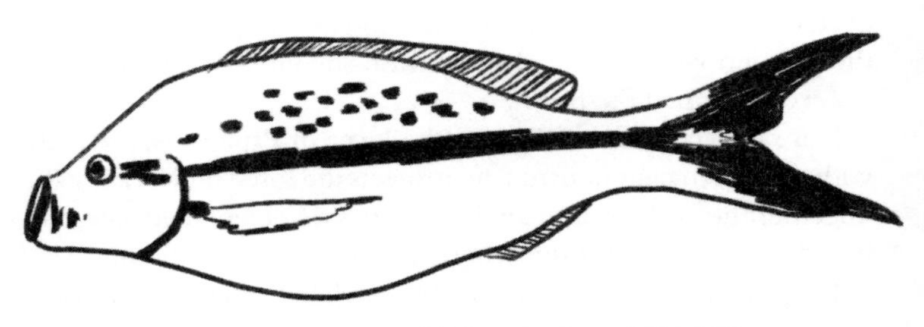

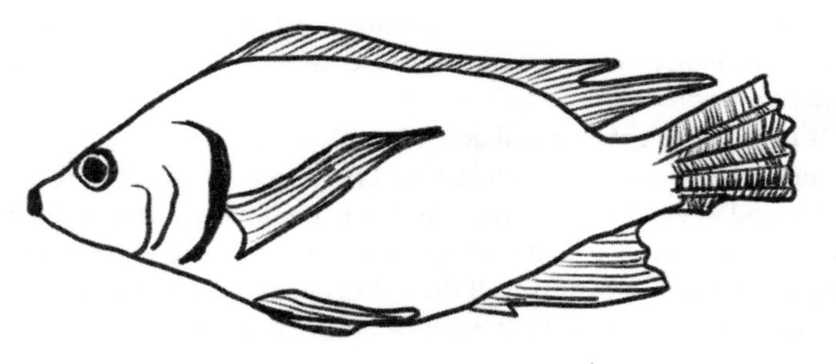

go and the next day his net was filled with shimmering fish, wriggling and recoiling as he pulled them in.

Overjoyed at his bounty, Tomas sold the fish in the market the next day. People marvelled at his plentiful catch, fish with scales the full spectrum of the rainbow. Bluefish, yellowtail snapper, silver tilapia. Word soon spread that Tomas sold the best variety of fish.

'From where do you get your fish Mrs Jacobs? What a nice size these are.' Aunt Flori, licked her fingers after eating some fry fish at her neighbour's house.

'Why thank you Aunt Flori. I travel all the way to Mayo village market to buy from Tomas the fisherman. He has fish as long as your arm!' she exclaimed, stretching out her hands in exaggeration.

People travelled from neighbouring villages to buy from Tomas and he continued to set his traps at night when he thought no one was around. Except someone was.

Mama D'leau was biding her time down below the surface of the river. She sat in her underwater kingdom, resplendent with palaces of glittering coral reefs and seagrass. fairymaids circled her golden throne, waiting to do her bidding. Mama D'leau's eyes shone with vengeance. She cracked her long, blue serpent's tail like a horsewhip and chose one of the fairymaids to deliver a curse to Tomas:

> Fairymaid, go and tell that greedy man to let my river be.
> There are plenty of fish in the ocean and plenty of fish in the sea.
> If I catch him anywhere near my river bed,
> I gon' lash him for all eternity and
> Mek him wish he was dead.

That very night when Tomas visited his spot by the river bank, he saw the silhouette of a woman with her back to him, lounging on the rocks. She was combing her thick locks of black hair with a golden comb, lined with sparkling jewels that glinted at him through the darkness. He could not see her face but his eyes traced the outline of her body, which curved down from her hips into the shape of a giant fishtail. He could barely believe his eyes.

All of the stories his family had told him were true. Here was a fairymaid with precious jewels in her hand. His mind raced ahead to all of the wealth he could gain by capturing her. He approached as quietly as he could and held out his long fishing hook to grab her by the hair.

'Stop where you are Tomas of Mayo village.' Her voice sliced through the air, halting his stride. She turned and held him in her steely gaze. 'I come with a message from Mama D'leau, protector of the rivers and all the creatures below.' She delivered the curse and prepared to dive back into the river. Tomas did not care about the threat of Mama D'leau. He was transfixed by the fairymaid and had to have her. He lunged at her with his fish hook, which grabbed onto her hair. He began to wind the hair tightly around his hook as he walked towards her. In an instant the fairymaid shapeshifted and transformed into a hissing, snarling black cat. With outstretched claws, she sprang on to Tomas's shoulder. He grabbed her by the body and was about to shove her into his bag when she shapeshifted again into a trickling stream of water that slid back into the river, fleeing right before his eyes.

Tomas was furious with himself that he had not caught the fairymaid. He spent the next few days plotting about all the various traps he could lay.

'Maybe I could lower a cage down into the river and she'll swim into it?' he thought. 'I could hang a net over the trees, ready to drop if she sits on the rocks down below.' He became obsessed with his new goal and focused on nothing else. He was oblivious to what was happening in his village. People were becoming sick. One by one, men, women and children were finding themselves confined to bed with a terrible fever. Soon, people in neighbouring villages became ill and the symptoms were similar. After eating a meal of fish, they felt violently sick, vomiting up all that they had eaten. Their next few days were spent with a raging fever of hot and cold chills.

The sickness spread across the island, twisting and turning in the direction of the sea breeze. Shops and schools were closed, parks were empty and markets were soulless without the banter of bargaining villagers. Fishermen were the only sellers untouched by the illness. They sat under umbrellas on their stalls, sheltering from the scorching sun. An abundance of fish left over at the end of each market day meant no money was made. No one was buying or eating fish. One evening, the fishermen gathered together by the sea wall to discuss what could be done. The tide drifted in, bringing the salty air and gentle sounds of lapping waves to mingle with their terrified voices.

'What are we going to do? Everyone who eats fish gets sick.'

'We're not sick. It can't be the fish.'

'There's a curse on us fisherman,' said one old man, who had lived through many unexplained events.

'Why would we be cursed? Who have we angered?' they cried. Many turned their backs and dismissed the old man.

'My grandson Tomas has been fishing in the river. Draining it of all the wildlife.' Suddenly he had their attention as he reminded them of the curse of Mama D'leau. Tomas waved his hand away when the men rounded on him, raising their voices and accusing him of bringing a curse upon all of their heads.

'You need to stop fishing in the river, for all of our sakes,' muttered his grandfather. The meeting came to a close with no resolution. Tomas stormed off, with thoughts of the fairymaid filling his mind.

The next morning he set off early before sunrise while the red howler monkeys were bellowing in the trees. The sea was calm and the dark, murky waters surrounded his tiny boat. With only a hanging light to forge his way in the darkness, Tomas headed towards a small lagoon where he thought something or someone was languishing on the rocks. His eyes had not deceived him, it was indeed the fairymaid, who had crept out from a waterfall cave.

He was overjoyed and quickly grabbed his long stick, which he'd fashioned into a harpoon with a sharp metal spear tied at the end. He stood up and threw the harpoon at the fairymaid's heart, piercing her naked flesh. Silence. And then the brittle crunch of her bones, breaking under the weight of his weapon.

Tomas lost his balance as the sea began to swirl around him. The calm waters were suddenly roaring with giant white-capped waves gathering pace in the distance. He grabbed onto the mast of his boat as it rocked violently from side to side and then he saw her. Emerging from the depths of the sea, Mama D'leau came charging towards him on the crest of a wave. Her long, black dreadlocks were twisting and thrashing, like vicious snakes around her head. Tomas closed his eyes and heard the deafening CRACK of a whip, as her long serpent tail buffeted the sea.

'Tomas your ears are too hard, so now you gone feel,' Mama D'leau called out above the sound of the waves, reminding him that he refused to listen to her warning and now he would pay the price. She raised up her heavy serpent tail and lashed it down upon his boat, splitting it in two.

Tomas fell into the water, kicking his legs and fighting to reach the surface. He clutched a raft of floating wood as the waves battered him from every direction. Saltwater poured into his eyes and lungs, stinging him with merciless venom. Mama D'leau twisted her heavy tail around him, snapping his body into tiny splinters, which she threw to all corners of the island.

'Since you ain't as you were, let you stay as you are,' she hissed before sinking back down to the depths of her underwater kingdom, carrying the lifeless body of the fairymaid with her.

It is said that the curse was lifted from the island that day. Health came back to the people who had been eating the river fish and trust was gradually restored in the fishermen and their bounty.

Tomas's boat was never found and he was never heard from again. Some say that he found his fame and fortune elsewhere. His grandfather says that Mama D'leau exacted her price for fouling the river and harming its creatures.

Stepped on a pin, the pin bent, and that's the way the story went.

Winston Nzinga, Jamaica

Professional Storyteller and Musician

I came to England in May 1965 with my three older sisters. We were coming to join our parents, who were in the UK already. I was only 6 years old. I always say to people, I'm Jamaican up to my knee! We left rural Jamaica on an open-backed truck that you put cattle in. It was rammed with people going to the airport.

We flew on the British Overseas Airways Corporation (BOAC) flight. This was my first time on an airplane. I looked out from the window as we were lowering to land at Heathrow, and there were lots of tiny things moving around on the ground below. They looked like tiny toys from the plane. I remember thinking, 'I'd like one of those.' It wasn't until I came out of the airport I saw they were in fact life-sized cars, not toys. I had never seen a car before.

My dad came to England first, with a five-year plan to save and go back like many others. His brother was here as well but they never realised how hard it was going to be for them. Britain was openly racist back then. It was at its peak during those years. It was hard to get on so he sent for my mum, so they could both work and eventually buy their own home. They needed to own their own property because whenever they went to rent somewhere, they were often confronted with signs in windows: 'No Blacks. No Irish. No Dogs.' No one wanted to rent a decent room to them. My parents thought, we were invited to come here.

We were asked to come by the government to help rebuild post-war Britain. The irony is that people were not prepared for us to come. The government did not pave the way. My dad started out as a labourer and then became an auxiliary nurse with people who needed psychiatric help. I remember him telling me there were even children in the hospital who were only there because they were illegitimate. My mum was also a nurse and she worked with geriatric people. I worked as a nurse for a while with children. I was one of four males, and the only one of African origin. The children loved me. I was only 18 years old at the time.

I grew up in Bristol, which is where my parents first settled. People used to comment on my accent. At home, around 9 years old, I tried to speak with an English accent so loudly in the house as I hoped people would hear it outside and imagine that English people were living inside.

I was never racially abused but there were areas you knew you couldn't walk. There were certain areas of Bristol that you knew as a black person, you were not safe. Some of the Jamaican boys were not going to stand for it. They got together as a crew and went into these 'white areas' and they beat those Bristol boys down who wouldn't let us walk certain streets. They made it safe for the rest of us younger boys.

My long-time memory from those days was the deep snow. At least 1m-deep snow. Despite the hardships at the time, there was definitely a community spirit. Everyone helped each other out. When snow fell on the ground, everybody came out and cleared their area of the pavement. People worked collectively to get things done. That's my abiding memory from the 1960s.

We were never taught about our black history in school here in the UK. I started reading and researching myself and that's what led to me changing my surname from Lewis to Nzinga. I found out about Queen Nzinga from Angola. In the late seventeenth century she resisted invasion from the Portuguese and fought against the slave trade for thirty years during her reign. I liked what she stood for. I like the name Nzinga, which means 'circle'. It's a Bantu name. The philosophy behind it is that anything within the circle is rich in spirit. It has no beginning and no end.

Storytelling and African drumming have always been a part of my life. In Jamaica, stories were told in the evenings on the veranda. After work we'd all socialise outside with stories and songs. My grandma was too old to go to church and so the church would come to our house. They would come and play the African drums. That was my first experience of hearing drumming. It was all part of Pukkumina, the Afro-Jamaican religion retained from the surviving African Kumina practices that had been brought to the island by enslaved Kongo people. My grandmother was into Pukkumina. This music and dance stayed in my blood. I was always tapping out rhythms at school. I became the lead drummer in the Boys' Brigade before I was scouted and invited to learn African drumming, which I use in my storytelling today.

Elma Holdip, Barbados

Nurse, Mother and Grandmother

I lived in St Michaels, Barbados and I grew up with storytelling. My family had a regular gospel meeting at our house and I remember the African drumming and wonderful songs that were always part of the stories. We would listen and dance. The house was often filled with music and songs.

I applied for a job in nursing when I was still in Barbados. I remember that they were asking for nurses to come over to England. I was young and happy for the adventure so I thought why not? I came to England in the early 1950s when I was 25 years old. I travelled to England on a ship and it took ten days. It was such a long time to travel. I came by myself and my brother came a few months later. I came to be a nurse and worked in Whittington Hospital. I remember earning £10 a month and I lived in. You could do that then. There were lots of girls from Trinidad working with me. Everyone was friendly to me, including the patients. But it was freezing.

It was so cold that I would stand in front of the fire in sister's office and one day I stood so close that I nearly went up in flames. I got terribly burnt from the fire and spent many weeks in hospital recovering. It was quite a hard time for me. Later on, I worked at the General Hospital and the Park Royal.

I stayed in nursing for many years until my daughter started school and then I stopped so that I could focus on being a mum.

Music & Song

These stories have been passed down orally and are meant to be spoken out loud. Lyrics and songs are central to the stories and I've created a few of my own right here. Variations of these stories have kept people's spirits alive in dark times across the islands, giving them hope when it seemed there was none.

THE SINGING BONES

Haiti

Many years ago, there lived a wealthy King whose kingdom sprawled across the highest peak of rugged mountains on Morne la Selle. Despite all of his wealth, money and treasures had lost their shine for him. He barely noticed the golden goblets or stores of diamonds. They piled up after each raid and after each tax was paid to him. Known for his love of rhythm and music, he found happiness in hearing songs and instruments being played.

Within the walls of his fortressed land, people were encouraged to dance and sing for the joy it would bring them. Whether it was a solemn wake to mourn the death of a loved one or a dance, everyone would celebrate in style. It was a wonderful sight to behold. Limbs bending and twisting beneath sticks, chests pulsating to the rhythms of their spirit. Bright, bold colours could be seen draped across bodies, stamping and roaring in time to the drums.

The start of the year was always a special day for the King. It was his birthday and yet in this particular year, he had become tired of the usual decadence of such occasions. Even preparations for the royal feast could not bring a smile to his face. The pigs had been slaughtered, seasoned and fried. The black rice had been boiled with mushrooms and peas. His favourite pumpkin and chilli soup, which was only allowed to be eaten by royalty, stared blankly back at him.

His mind went wandering through all of his accomplishments hoping to cheer himself up: 'I have riches beyond anyone's imagination. I am loved and respected by my people. I rule over many.' Despite all of these accolades, he felt numb, even bored of hearing it. He wanted something new to experience, some way of validating his worth. An idea soon occurred to him. The King turned to his only son and daughter and asked them to take part in a competition.

'I'd like each of you to perform your best talent for me,' he announced, without asking their opinion. 'Whoever shines the brightest and pleases me the most, shall inherit the kingdom when I am gone.' His daughter smiled and bowed her head. Her dark braids shimmered with golden thread laced through each one. Her face, the colour of tamarind wood, shone with nature's gentle manner. She was blessed with a singing voice that fluttered faster than hummingbirds and soared past the island's volcanic peaks. But her brother, well, he clenched his fist and bit his lip until he drew blood. Unlike his sister, he had no obvious talent to speak of and saw no reason why his birthright should be gambled away. His envy snaked around the room like deadly vipers about to strike. He could not refuse and risk looking weak to his father. And so it was agreed. There was to be a talent contest between the two royal heirs.

That very night, the King sat in his palace courtyard beneath the swaying palm trees, surrounded by guards, advisors, and local onlookers. His daughter stood on one of the upper-floor balconies and began to sing. Her voice commanded everyone's attention, even the stars in the sky. She sang of her home 'the pearl of the Antilles' with its sloping mountain curves and tropical forests. When she finished, the King praised her for filling their hearts with song and spoke of his eagerness to see what his son would perform the next day.

Early the next morning, the King's daughter strolled through the forest looking for flowers to pick for her father. She knew how much he loved the scarlet hibiscus. As she walked between

the giant tree ferns, she heard twigs snap behind her. She turned around and saw her brother.

'Brother dear, you startled me.' She held up her arms to show him the flowers and then saw something ghastly in his eyes. Some say she saw her own death. She shrieked and shrank back into the bushes. He grabbed her by the neck, twisting his fingers tightly around it and squeezing with all his might. Her arms grasped at his face, clawing and scratching desperately to make him stop, but it was of little use. Like a fragile twig, snapped carelessly in two, she fell limp into his arms. He took her lifeless body and buried it under a wild bayawon tree where only the leaves could whisper of the murder they had seen.

You might think that he would act strangely after committing such a deed. Maybe he would seem anxious or guilty? But no. The King's son swaggered back to the palace and raised not even an eyebrow when guards were sent to look for his missing sister. The hunt went on for days, weeks, months but no trace of her was found. The King was distraught, as you would expect him to be. His spirit was broken and nothing gave him any joy. Music and song were no longer heard around the kingdom. It vanished with his daughter.

Until one day, a farmer was in the bush, walking with his dog. He swung his arms high, hacking at leaves with his machete to clear a path. His dog started barking and sniffing at the roots of a tree. The farmer couldn't see anything there but his dog kept barking and digging furiously, kicking up the soil. There, near the surface was a bone that he grabbed between his sharp teeth, wagging his tail with delight. The farmer was horrified, suspecting it to be a human bone. He took it from his dog's mouth and as he examined it, the bone began to sing:

Farmer, farmer, do you know?
My bones are buried down below.
My brother killed me for the crown.
He took my life without a sound.
My bones lay under a bayawon tree,
Farmer, farmer, set me free.

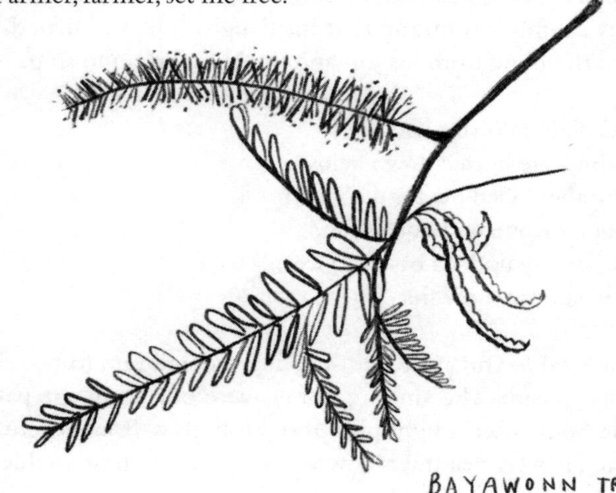

The farmer could barely believe his ears but knew exactly what he had to do. He headed straight to the palace and begged to see the King. Remember I said that these were dark times? An audience with the King was no longer easy. He refused to see anyone, wanting to be left alone and kept himself hidden behind his palace shutters.

His son heard the farmer shouting, insisting on seeing the King, and wondered what all the commotion was. He bellowed, 'What is it that you want farmer? Why are you here?' The farmer did not want to get into any trouble. He bowed down respectfully before the Prince and handed him the bone. And once more, the bone began to sing:

Brother, brother do you know?
My bones are buried down below.
You have killed me for the crown.
You took my life without a sound.
My bones lay under a bayawon tree,
Brother, brother, set me free.

The melodious voice from the singing bone was unmistakable. Like the gentle rise of the morning sun, her voice warmed the dark corners of the palace and brought light to the King. He rose from his chamber thinking that his daughter had returned. He snatched the bone from his son and the bone began to sing:

Father, father do you know?
My bones are buried down below.
My brother killed me for the crown.
He took my life without a sound.
My bones lay under a bayawon tree,
Father, father, set me free.

The son tried to run away but the King ordered him to be seized and put to death. The singing bones were buried in the palace grounds. Soon after, a light pink rose bush grew from where her bones lay. They say that this is how we come to have roses to this day.

When the Paths Vanished

Cuba

It was a glorious day in Cuba, like any other. Sunshine spread its rays into every corner, making the plants bloom and grow. Coffee was ready for harvesting, fruits were ripe for picking and people greeted each other with their usual warmth and optimism, while setting off to work. That's when they noticed that the roads had closed. All of the paths across the island leading to other villages and the coast had suddenly vanished overnight.

In their place grew a forest with thick, wild grass towering over 30ft high. It was believed by the people that Iku, the Yoruba dark spirit of Death, was blocking the paths. He was guarding the roads and making it impossible to pass. If you attempted to cross through the tightly knitted branches of grass, you would be taken by Iku and never seen again.

Everyone, everywhere was trapped. People in the north of the country who had been visiting from the south could no longer return to their homes. Neighbours wanting to spend time with friends elsewhere could no longer see them. It was a complete lockdown across the island. Feelings of despair and isolation soon grew in people's hearts, with thoughts of escape dominating their minds. Those who did leave, never returned. They were feared dead, captured by Death.

After a while, time ceased to exist. Celebrations and events felt weary and pointless without any future hope of change. Those from the coast that were trapped in the hills, wept at the sound of the wind rustling through the trees, for it reminded them of waves crashing in the sea. Those from the hillside, marooned by the coast, were tormented by the sound of the sea breeze, for it carried memories of the forest sounds, gently whispering from the shore.

Time passed, as time does with villages turning to decay. Gardens were no longer maintained and buildings were rotting with disrepair. Most people had vanished along with the paths but an old couple remained in the eastern village of Baracoa. Surrounded by sweet-smelling cacao trees and coffee plants, they nurtured the land and each other.

Together they had twenty children over the years. Boys and girls with wavy dark hair and skin the colour of cinnamon bark. They brought so much joy to their parents and other villagers who were old enough to remember a time when they were free to roam. But eventually each child grew up and wanted to leave their home.

They'd turn to their parents and say, 'I want to know what is beyond this village. I need to find out for myself.' No matter how much their parents begged them to stay, they all eventually vanished into the haze of overgrown bush and were never seen again.

The couple had finally resolved to live out their elderly years without the comfort of their children, when a truly magical thing happened. The old woman gave birth again. This time to identical twin boys who they named Taewo and Kainde. The elders in the village called the boys *ibelles* – sacred twins – and praised the African gods for their arrival.

'The powerful *orisha* Obatala has breathed life into them,' they all agreed, knowing that somehow the village had been blessed by their birth. Everyone felt a renewed sense of hope. The boys were doted upon by all of the women in the village, who loved them as much as their own sons. Their supple bodies and hair were smoothed daily with coconut oil. They grew tall and strong, fed on a diet of viandas of green plantain, cassava and sweet potatoes.

It was impossible to tell the twins apart. They were like two cocoa beans in a pod. If you looked closely, you could see that Taewo, the youngest, had eyes the colour of dark coffee whilst Kainde's eyes were a reddish shade of mahogany. A soft light shimmered from their smiling faces, which people felt was a divine mark that signalled the good fortune they would bring.

'Olorun the sky *orisha* who holds up the heavens, is protecting our *ibelles*,' they'd say whenever they passed by. Cheeky and mischievous, the boys played tricks on anyone who could not tell them apart.

'No, that was Taewo who promised to help you mend the chair, I am Kainde,' he giggled to his neighbour, cupping his hands around his mouth to cover rows of dazzling white teeth.

One day, just like their siblings before them, Taewo and Kainde turned to their parents and said, 'We want to know what is beyond this village. We need to go and find out for ourselves.' Their parents were devastated.

'Nooo, not my *ibelles*, I cannot bear it,' wailed their mother, beating the earth with her fists. Pain and sorrow threatened to seep through the village again until one of the elders spoke up. 'Let us rejoice in their bravery and hold a fiesta to wish the twins good luck on their way.'

The women sashayed out in their long Bata Cubana dresses, layered with cherry red, sunrise orange and white ruffled edges. They twirled around and formed a circle. The twins stood in the middle wearing their white cotton guayaberas and shorts. People danced up to them and placed lime-green guava fruit in their deep pockets for their journey. Everyone waved long palm leaves in the air and sang:

Shine *ibelles*, shine
Let the paths open up for you.
Shake *ibelles*, shake
Let the sun and moon guard you.

Taewo and Kainde kissed their parents goodbye and walked into the forest. The thick grass parted for them, opening up the path so that they could easily make their way. It then closed up right behind them so that no one else could get through. The paths vanished again.

Protected by their shimmering light, the boys marched north for seven days in the direction of the coast. Their plan was to walk along the edge of the island and see if any of the paths to other villages would open up for them. They strolled over rocky hills abundant with black walnut trees, stopping only to eat the rice and beans their mother had packed. At night they slept under the stars, undisturbed by the scratching sound of critters who crept out to feed.

On the eighth day they reached the island coast and saw the vast sea for the first time in their lives. Their eyes stretched to the edge of the horizon and they gasped in awe and wonder at the sight. A light blue canvas of sky dotted with white clouds was mirrored in the crystal clear waters beneath it. Taewo turned to his brother and said: 'Look! The sky is touching the water. There is no end to the sea. It goes on forever.'

They stood still and felt the sea breeze caress their faces, and listened to the gentle sh-sh-sh of the waves rolling in. It was their first taste of freedom and they wanted to run down the hill and dive into the water but another sound interrupted this reverie. It sounded like a hundred frogs croaking followed by the sound of a hundred horses shuddering down below.

They looked down the hillside and saw a long stretch of golden sand littered with human bones. Skulls, arms, legs and spines were piled on top of each other, surrounding the enormous body of a giant beast. The ghastly sounds were coming from him. He was slumped on his side, sleeping with his cavernous mouth wide open, and snoring loudly. The foul stench of rotting flesh drifted in their direction with each exhale. The giant was Okurri Boroku. He was the devil who had closed up all of the roads and his colossal body was stretched across the beach, blocking their way.

'Look at the size of that giant. His legs are thick like gnarly tree trunks and his enormous body could fill our whole house.' Taewo stared in amazement.

'What a STINK,' Kainde pinched his nose to mask the smell. 'How will we get past him?' he asked his brother, worried that their bones would end up on the pile with the others who had got this far. There was no way that they could cross to the other side of the island without waking him up.

'Quick, don't let him see us,' said Taewo, tugging his brother's arm. They crouched down in the grass and stared at this unsightly giant. His boulder-sized head was covered with red feathers hanging from a mass of tangled hair. One eye was closed and the other was bulging slightly open, revealing a black pupil that stared out blankly. Occasionally he lifted his heavy arm and swatted away mosquitos buzzing around his face.

'I will rouse him,' said Taewo. 'You lie low and stay here.' He marched down the hill, whistling as he went, expecting the giant to wake up and roar. But he didn't. He carried on sleeping and snoring heavily.

'WAKE UP!' yelled Taewo. 'You are in my way. I want to pass.' He stood with his hands on his hips, staring straight at the devil. Okurri Boroku lazily lifted one eye and closed it again. It was clear to Taewo that he would not stir easily. Perhaps he has been sleeping for many years, he thought. He lifted his foot and kicked the giant's arm.

'GET UP!' yelled Taewo again. This time he pulled the devil's feathers on his head and then jumped back to a safe distance.

Okurri Boroku opened his eyes and saw the *ibelle* standing before him. He stood up slowly, yawned loudly and looked down at Taewo. 'What are you doing here boy? Do you know who I am?' he roared, revealing long jagged teeth that flashed like spears in his mouth.

Taewo smiled sweetly. 'I would like to pass please. You are in my way.'

'Look at my teeth boy. I am hungry. I have not had any people to eat for a long time.' The giant looked him over from head to toe.

Taewo stood his ground. He barely came up to the height of the giant's waist. 'You need to let me pass. You need to let everyone pass.' His voice remained firm as he stared defiantly into Okurri

Boroku's dark eyes. The devil, chuckled, admiring Taewo's bravery. Perhaps I could have some fun with this boy, before I devour him, he thought to himself.

He turned to Taewo and offered him a challenge.

'I like to dance, boy. It's been a long time since I have danced.' He handed Taewo a tall, barrel-shaped makuta drum. 'Play this drum and if I like your rhythm, I will dance. Play and we will see who grows tired first. If I stop, then you shall pass. But if you stop, then I shall eat you up and your bones can join the others.' Okurri Boroku threw back his head and howled with laughter.

Taewo took the makuta drum and climbed up the hillside, near where his brother was crouching. 'I shall play from here while you dance.' He then slapped his open hands on the drum one at a time, sending loud beats soaring into the sky:

Ka, ka ka, ka taa
Ka, ka ka, ka taa

The devil lifted up his feet and began to dance. He stamped in the sand and swung his long arms at the side of his waist. He shook his head from side to side, making the bright red feathers in his hair twist around.

'I like it! Play boy, play,' growled the devil. Taewo increased his rhythm, hitting the drum with the edge of his hand, then slapping it with the other. The devil danced furiously, urging him to carry on. He danced for hours, swinging his hips and shrugging his shoulders in time to the beat. Taewo's hands continued drumming until they were stinging, red raw with pain.

His brother lay on his tummy watching through the tall blades of grass. He crawled along, inch by inch until he was right beside Taewo's feet. He waited patiently for a sign to take over. The sun began to set, drawing a blanket of darkness across the sky. The devil twirled around and when his back faced the boys, Kainde sprung up from the grass and Taewo dropped down. They exchanged places without the devil seeing. Kainde continued to play the drum with all his might.

'Dance devil dance. Dance until you drop,' he sang, slapping the drum even faster. Smoke poured out from Okurri Boroku's nostrils and ears as he spun around wildly. Birds of darkness joined in the dance, with night owls screeching and winged bats flapping around the devil's head.

Taewo had crawled away into the hillside and was hiding behind a tree where he could rest and drink water without being seen. This went on for two days and two nights, with the *ibelles* switching places while the devil danced to the beat of the drum.

Finally on the third day, when the sun reached its highest peak, his feet began to slow down. Sweat dripped down the sides of his face and venomous blood leaked from his eyes and ears. He wanted the drum to stop beating so he could stop dancing. His body ached and his strength ebbed away in the merciless heat.

Still the devil danced on into the night with his breath laboured and his voice hoarse. He croaked, 'Play boy, play.' When he uttered those last words, his body swayed backwards and he dropped down dead onto the sand.

The *ibelles* ran down the hillside and circled his body. 'Your curse is lifted Okurri Boroku. This is our time,' they said. And they were right. With the devil now defeated, the paths opened up. The knotted blades of bush and grass drew back and the roads appeared.

The twins climbed up high into a silk cotton tree, also known as the tree of life and home to all spirits. They sat amidst its majestic branches, over 200ft high above the ground, and called out to the *orisha* Obatala. 'Restore the lives of the people taken by Okurri Boroku. Bring back their souls once more.' Their voices rang out into the night sky, where their prayer was heard by the powerful spirit.

In the valley below, the spirits took up their bones lying scattered along the paths that had been closed by Okurri Boroku. They breathed life into their bodies and returned to their families and homes. The *ibelles* had conquered the devil and brought love and light back to the island. To this day, *ibelles* are seen as the guardians of the paths. Their presence ensures that peace will always be maintained.

The Guitar Player

Grenada

Around the same time every year, the rhythm of love floats in on the sea breeze and dances around the island. Calypso beats keep it moving in time and everyone is feeling lively and ready to celebrate. As you move through the streets, passing brightly painted houses with open doors and windows, you'll catch the sweet smell of black fruit cakes with cinnamon spices and dried fruits dripping with year-old wine and rum.

This is the start of the wedding season on the islands. Dance halls are lit up each night with wedding parties and bands entertaining the guests. On one of these nights, Johnny was asked to play his guitar for a wedding near Flamingo Bay, where the houses overlook the narrow harbour and deep blue waters. He'd been booked to join the band and he was eager to taste a delicious free meal and have a chance to sweet talk the ladies.

During the evening, a young woman in a flowing, yellow dress caught his eye. He began to strum his strings as if only for her. She matched his tempo with her body, swaying and fluttering her arms like a mockingbird in flight. She smiled, knowing that he was watching her but never met his eyes.

This went on long into the night and as the guests began to peel away, Johnny finally spoke to the beautiful woman he'd been playing his guitar for. Her name was Clarissa and she was a cousin of the bride. Johnny complimented her hazel eyes and the yellow bell flowers tied into her hair. She blushed and returned the compliment.

'Thank you Johnny. I loved hearing your music tonight. It made me feel as free as a bird,' she said and spun around on her red heels to show she wished the music could go on. He wanted to spend more time with her too and offered to walk her home, seeing as it was now past midnight and her friends had gone home. They left the party together, walking side by side.

The night air was cool and the moonlit roads were empty. Only the crickets could be heard creaking in the distance. As

they walked, Johnny strummed on his guitar to serenade his new love:

> Meet me down by the river
> Come when the sun rise up high
> Meet me down by the river
> Hear the songbirds in the sky

Clarissa listened to Johnny's melody, linking her arm through his as they made their way in the darkness. She was glad to have his music take her mind off any thoughts about jumbies on the road. She'd been told the stories about spirits who walk the streets at night and so she kept her eyes firmly fixed ahead.

The road was barely lit up, with only the occasional street lamp. Darkness closed in on either side of them like a silent pack of wolves, waiting to pounce. Red eyes blinked from the night owls, who hovered in branches. Occasionally bats scattered their wings across the night sky. Johnny was still strumming his guitar gently but Clarissa was finding it hard not to let her imagination run away with her into the shadows.

The wedding hall was now way behind them and they came upon a long bridge that took them to Mount Moritz Road, which circled around her parish. She stopped walking abruptly and cocked her head to one side. Listening intently.

'Can you hear that music?' she asked fearfully. Johnny laughed and carried on playing. 'Of course, I can hear my own music. Don't you like it?' he asked, worried that his charm was now wearing off.

'Not your music. Listen. Listen to that sound,' she whispered, shaking him by the arm until he stopped playing his guitar. Johnny stopped playing and wondered what had gotten into her. She had seemed so pleasant earlier. Then he heard it. There was the sound of another guitar playing further away from them in the distance.

Johnny smiled with relief. Perhaps it was someone else from the band up ahead. 'Come let's find out who it is there. Maybe we can both sing to you all the way home,' he held her hand and they carried on walking across the bridge, towards the sound of a mournful melody.

Lit up by the light of the moon, the figure of a man came into view. He was sitting at the end of the bridge, strumming gently, his bleak voice drifting towards them. Johnny didn't recognise him but whoever he was, he seemed harmless enough. Clarissa shivered and held his hand tightly. She didn't feel comfortable and wasn't sure why. Johnny urged her on, 'Come, let's see who he is.'

As they approached, the man didn't stop playing or singing. His face was partially hidden by a straw hat, frayed around the edges. His expression looked weary and etched with sorrow.

'Good evening,' said Johnny. 'Have you come from the wedding?'

As soon as the question left his lips, he knew the answer. This man was barefoot and dressed in very old, tatty clothing. His trousers had holes and he was wearing a cotton blouse, cut in a style that no one wore anymore. He did not look like someone who had just been at a party.

They decided to walk on and leave him at the side of the bridge. Just then, the most peculiar thing happened. As they began to walk ahead, they were somehow back at the start of the bridge, where they had just come from.

'What is happening?' Clarissa cried. She clutched Johnny's arm and they walked faster, almost running across the bridge. The guitar player continued to play his melancholy tune but as they drew closer to him, his music became a frantic pace. His fingers scurried like tarantulas across the frets and his voice took on a strength that seemed larger than life.

Johnny had never seen such musicality. He wanted to hear more but knew they should just keep going. As they hurried past the man, they found themselves at the start of the bridge again. Somehow they were in a continuous time loop.

Johnny grabbed Clarissa by the arm and turned back towards the wedding venue. He hoped they could find another way home but as they turned, they ended up facing the guitar player again on his side of the bridge.

'What's going on man?' yelled Johnny. He shielded Clarissa with his body and she clung to his back, hoping she was in a dream. The man stopped playing and for the first time, looked up at them both. His eyes were filled with tears that did not fall down his cheeks. Clarissa saw the line of a deep bruise across his throat that looked like the mark made from a rope. He stared blankly at her and said, 'You shouldn't be out this late at night.' His voice was raspy and hoarse.

'We know. We're just trying to get home,' Johnny almost pleaded, hoping the man would help them, but he did not reply. Johnny decided to try a different approach with him. 'You play guitar so well. I've never heard anything like it,' he offered, sounding as casual as he could.

'Thank you,' said the man. 'You should have heard me play when I was alive.'

The Singing Sack

Guyana

The same trick won't serve a man twice – Caribbean proverb

There once was a young girl named Eleanor with skin the colour of ripe cacao beans. She wore a broad, welcoming smile buried deep within her cheeks and lived with her family in a home nestled in the highlands of Guyana, surrounded by sloping hills and far-reaching forests.

Each day, before the sun had fully risen in the sky, Eleanor began her household tasks. She'd reach for the cocoyea broom

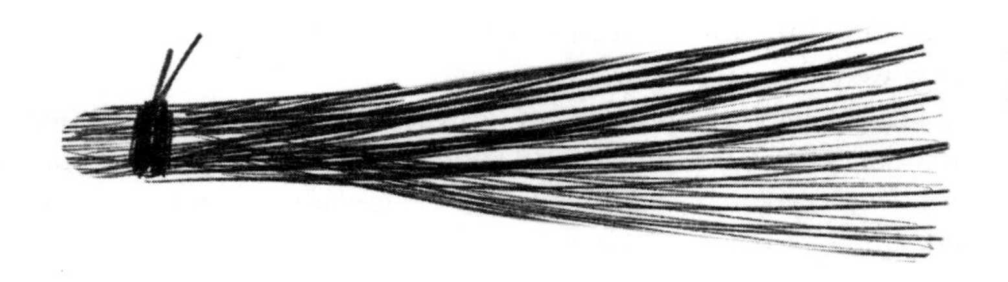

and sing softly to herself as she swept the dust out of the house. She glided from room to room, swaying and swishing with the broom's long leaves. Her voice sounded like a sprinkle of sunshine, each word warming your heart as you listened:

> I sing to let the daylight in,
> Let the daylight in.
> I sweep to clear the shadows away,
> Clear the shadows away.

Eleanor's family loved to hear her sing. Her mother and brothers listened, as her voice floated into every room of their tiny house, filling it with joy.

One morning, after sweeping from the front to the back of the house, she headed out to their yard to feed the chickens. The birds clucked and puffed up their feathers, as soon as they heard her coming. They knew their breakfast was near.

'Morning everyone,' she sang, scattering kernels of corn onto the ground. They cooed even more loudly, poking their beaks into the earth in all directions. Next she went behind her house, into the field to pick golden oranges. The trees were clustered together with bunches of sweet-smelling fruit, dangling from their branches.

Eleanor's singing soared high into the air and greeted the birds, who were circling and diving up above. She sang while piling her basket high with fresh fruit.

This was how she spent most of her mornings and before long, the sun had reached its hottest, blazing heat upon her head. In the distance, Eleanor could hear the crashing sound of Kaieteur Falls, and she longed to bathe in its cool waters.

'Mother, please can I go and swim down by the river,' she pleaded, clasping her hands together in prayer. 'It's too hot to stay home.' Her mother tutted and shook her head. The river snaked through the middle of the forest, surrounded by silk cotton trees, believed to be where the spirits slept.

'You can't go alone and I'm heading into the village to sell these cakes. Your brothers won't be back before dark.'

Eleanor sighed, knowing that her mother wouldn't change her mind. So an entire afternoon yawned ahead of her, filled with sweltering heat and no way to cool down. But once she was alone, her heart felt brave and she decided to go for a short walk in the shade. She followed the path that curved along the bottom of the mountain, being careful not to head into the forest.

But perhaps it was the intoxicating smell of the pink and white lilies, scattered between the grass, or the flight of the ruby hummingbird, darting in between the trees. Whatever it was, Eleanor turned off the path and headed into the dense forest. Lost in song, she wandered past the iguanas hanging out upside down on their branches and the slow-moving sloths chewing through their leaves. She sang to the birds above and the creatures below, wandering deeper and deeper into the forest.

Also making his way nearby, was an old man whose heart was as crooked as his legs. He walked with the help of a long, black stick, carved from the branch of a crabwood tree.

Across his back, he carried a rough sack, ready to fill it with anything of value. He stumbled through the forest, cursing every stone or bush in his way, wishing each one would disappear. And then he heard it. A melody sweeter than any songbird. It echoed through the branches, and drifted down below the canopy of leaves. The old man stopped to listen. 'What a beautiful voice,' he thought, his mind racing to how he could make riches from it. 'People would pay generously to hear such singing.'

He walked steadily in the direction of the voice, tightening his hold on the sack. Eleanor had reached the river and was contemplating whether to stop for a while. The river gushed past, making its journey from the steep rocks.

'Oh dear, look how far I've come,' she said aloud, realising that she had disobeyed her mother and gone alone. If the trees could speak all the secrets from the spirits, they would have warned her to go swiftly back home. But the water looked inviting with silver fishes dancing beneath the surface.

'I'll just dip my feet in,' she thought and waded in slowly. The chill on her toes felt such a relief in the middle of the humid day. Soon she'd forgotten her promise to her mother and was swimming and splashing around, unaware that she was being watched.

The old man's face blended into the bark of a pine tree. He stood very still and peered out with narrow eyes at Eleanor. 'There is the song bird,' he declared and crouched down low out of sight. He watched and waited. His crooked knees began to ache and his back became weary but he was in no rush.

'If greedy wait, hot will cool,' he thought, believing that his patience would soon be rewarded.

When she came out of the water, Eleanor could not find one of her shoes. She poked around in the long grass, knowing that she had left them nearby. Her eyes looked up through the blades and saw two beady eyes staring back at her. She shrieked and fell back in surprise.

'Good afternoon. I did not know anyone was here,' she managed to stutter out. The old man stood up and moved closer.

'I have something that belongs to you,' he replied with a smile and held out one of her shoes. Eleanor relaxed and thanked him, taking the shoe from his hands, but as soon as they were on her feet, she felt a rough hand grab hold of her wrist. He opened his sack and threw her inside.

'Let me out!' she cried, wriggling and squirming, but all she heard was a quiet cackle in reply as he threw the sack over his back and marched out of the forest, with only the trees to witness what he had done. The old man walked through the night until he reached the next village. Early the next morning he arrived at a market square and positioned himself with his sack in the middle where everyone could see him. Slowly, men, women and children filled up the square, buying and selling for the day. The old man called out loudly for all to hear, 'Come here, come here and listen to my magical singing sack.'

People started to gather around him, watching and waiting for the show to begin. The old man bent down and whispered:

Sing, singing sack, sing!
Or with my stick I'll beat you.

From inside the sack, a sweet voice poured out mournfully:

Because I swam in the river, mother,
I was caught without my shoe
Because I swam in the river, mother
Never will I see you.

The crowd listened, spellbound by the magical sack and its melody. They clapped and cheered.

'Again! Again!'

'What a wonderful voice!'

The old man smiled a crooked smile to match his crooked stick and held out his hat to collect money from the people. The next day he moved to a different village, revealing his singing sack. Again the people marvelled at his magical trick and poured coins into his hat. The little girl wept each night and begged to go home but the old man always refused. He wandered from village to village and town to town putting on a show with his singing sack. And each time the people clapped and cheered, asking to hear more.

One evening, the old man came to a boarding house in the village where Eleanor was from. He sat at a table waiting to be fed with his sack placed beside him. His fame had now spread far and wide, and strangers staying at the house wanted to hear from the magical singing sack. The old man stood up and whispered to the sack:

Sing, singing sack, sing!
Or with my stick I'll beat you.

From inside the sack, a sweet voice poured out mournfully:

Because I swam in the river, mother,
I was caught without my shoe
Because I swam in the river, mother
Never will I see you.

Once again, the people cheered and marvelled at the magical sack. They clapped and asked for more. Among the crowd that evening was one of Eleanor's brothers, who worked in the kitchen. As he swept the floor, the sound of his sister's voice drifted into his ears and buried itself in his sorrowful heart.

At first he thought he was mistaken, missing his sister so much that perhaps he had dreamed up her voice. He listened again, drinking in all of the words, and decided that it was definitely her. He threw down his broom and went charging into the dining room, pushing and shoving past the jubilant crowd. There in the middle, stood the crooked old man, leaning on his crooked stick.

'Open the sack, let me see inside,' he growled with fury swelling in his eyes.

The old man refused, emboldened by his fame and the adoring crowd.

'This is a magic sack and it must stay closed to keep its secrets,' he sneered, twisting the sack firmly shut.

'Get back to the kitchen!' yelled the crowd. 'You're spoiling our show!' People complained and shooed him away but he was sure of what he heard. In one swift move, he grabbed open the sack and found Eleanor inside. For a moment it was as if time had stood still, the air was sucked out of the room with the sound of everyone's gasp. The magic of the sack was revealed for all to see and at once everyone knew what had happened.

Her brother grabbed the stick and chased the old man out of the village with all of the villagers howling and cheering right behind him.

Eleanor was happily reunited with her family and you can be sure that the crooked old man was never seen or heard from again.

Dance, Granny, Dance

Antigua

One fine day, when the sun was gently rolling out across the sky, Anansi found himself strolling through the village looking for food. His throat was dry and brittle. His stomach was concave, groaning with emptiness. Where am I going to find something to eat? He complained, scratching his chin. You see, that morning he woke up to the sound of his tummy rumbling and his wife cursing him.

'Anansi, what are you good for? Go and find us something to eat!' she hollered, tapping on his head as if it was an empty coconut shell. But still he did not stir. So she tugged at his feet.

'Anansi, get up! You're so lazy,' she said, hoping to encourage him out of his deep slumber. Finally, he peeped open one eye and saw his wife standing over him, hands on hips, glaring down with two beady eyes. He sat up straight, knowing that he wasn't going to get any more rest that day.

'Taking time out ain't laziness,' said Anansi, feeling slightly irritable at being woken up.

'Well, only the early bird gets the sweetest flower,' she answered back, and ushered him out of the house.

Anansi left reluctantly, promising not to come back without something to eat for the whole family. So that is how he came to be walking around sleepily, before the sun had fully settled in the sky.

On the side of the road, he passed Mrs Dunn, who was selling coconut water from her small stand. He stared longingly at the husky coconut shells with straws poking out for you to sip from. His mouth began to water at the thought of drinking some refreshing coconut juice.

'Hmm, that's exactly what I need to cool me down and quench my thirst,' He thought to himself and put on his best smile to greet her.

'Morning Mrs Dunn,' hailed Anansi. 'You got any free-ness for me today?' He asked, holding out his hands to beg.

'No Anansi. I'm not giving anything away for free,' she snapped, shaking her head at his nerve. She knew that he would not stop at just one drink. He shrugged it off and carried on his way. Further along, Anansi saw Mrs Clarke sitting beneath her bright red umbrella, which fanned out over her cake stall. The sweet smell of coconut and peanut drops drifted over, tickling his nose and making his belly rumble more. Oh how he wanted to crunch on one of the bars and chew on those toffee chunks. He stepped up confidently,

'Morning Mrs Clarke, you got any free-ness for me today?' He asked hopefully, presenting his broadest smile.

'No Anansi. Nothing for you today,' she said and turned her back towards him, knowing that he'd never stop at eating just one.

Things were not turning out exactly as he'd hoped. People were resisting his charm. But again, Anansi shrugged it off. To him, it only meant that something else better would turn up. He walked away from the cake stalls and headed out of the village to search for food or someone he could take it from.

'What I need is someone who has more food than sense,' he said aloud, looking all around him, but no one was about. He continued walking along the dirt path, hoping to bump into someone that he could beg for a little food.

By mid-morning, his feet were sore, his mouth was dry and his belly was still rumbling.

'What a sorry state I've found myself in. There's too many mouths in my house to feed,' he complained to himself, wiping sweat from his brow. He sat down beside a balata tree to rest for a while and think of how he could come up with some food. He'd barely closed his eyes when he heard joyful humming coming from one of the fields just ahead. Thinking that this might be someone who had food, Anansi got up to see who it was. He peered through the bush and his eyes nearly sprang from his head.

'Just look at all that food! ' he cried out. In front of him was a field covered in golden corn, stretching as far as his eyes could see. There at the edge of the corn rows, was Granny with her basket, humming softly to herself while picking the corn.

To the left of the field was an abundance of fruit trees. Red mango, yellow star fruit and lime-green guava, all dangling from their branches, ripening in the sunshine. He crouched down low, so that Granny would not see him. After all, he did not want to be dragged into doing any work. Anansi licked his lips and breathed in the sweet and sour smell from all the delicious fruits.

'There is enough food here to feed us for days,' he grinned widely, imagining his whole family crunching on roasted corn and sucking sweet mangoes. Granny was filling her basket, unaware that Anansi was watching. Her yellow straw hat shaded her face from the blazing sun and she carried on humming, happily collecting her corn. Anansi's mind started to form a plan. He needed to find a way to get hold of the corn without having to do any of the harvesting. He was far too lazy for that.

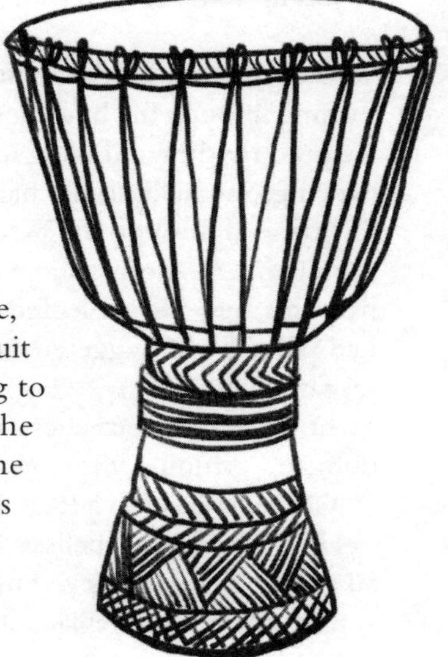

He climbed up into the balata tree, perched among its cherry-shaped fruit and pulled out his drum. I'm going to sing Granny such a sweet tune she won't be able to resist the music, he laughed to himself and opened his mouth to sing as loud as he could. He let his voice rise up into the cloudless sky.

Aye yay, yay yay.
Dance, Granny, dance.
Aye yay, yay yay.
Lift up your foot and dance.

As soon Granny's ears heard the base sound from the drum, her shoulders immediately started to move. Anansi beat down harder, playing faster and faster, letting his hands dictate the rhythm. Granny put down her basket and instantly wanted to dance. She couldn't help herself. As soon as she heard the music, her toes were tapping, her hips were swaying and her knees were bending. Her dark green skirt flared out around her and she glided gracefully like a parakeet bird, diving and swooping in time to the music.

'Oh, how I love to hear such tunes,' she said, jumping up and jumping down. Anansi sang louder:

Aye yay, yay yay.
Dance, Granny, dance.
Aye yay, yay yay.
Lift up your foot and dance.

The Caribbean breeze drifted in from the south, twisting and turning through the branches and the leaves. It gathered pace with Anansi's rhythm and blew into the cornfield where Granny was dancing. She held up her hands and let the winds carry her away. She danced through the fields and over the hills, way up into the mountains. As soon as she was out of sight, Anansi jumped down from his tree and collected all of the golden corn that Granny had picked. He staggered home laden with corn and surprised his family.

'Look what I have here for everyone!' he called out on his doorstep, grinning with pride.

'Come let us have a feast tonight.'

His wife couldn't believe her eyes. 'Anansi! Where did you get all of this corn?' She eyed him up suspiciously but that trickster was ready with his explanation.

'I've been working hard all day in the field, sweating under the sun, and now I need to put my feet up and eat.' He sat down and let his family fuss around him, happy that they could have a good meal that night. His wife roasted the corn and they all ate until their bellies were full.

Meanwhile, poor Granny was making her way back to her field. When she arrived, the sun had already dipped behind the trees and her basket of corn was gone.

'I don't know what came over me today but I know someone is up to no good.' She put it out of her mind and retired for the night.

The following day, Anansi couldn't wait to return to Granny's place. Those golden kernels tasted so sweet, he wanted more. 'What is Granny going to do with all that fruit and corn anyway? he said to himself. 'It's too much for her. I'm helping her out by taking it off her hands.'

He made his way to the field and found Granny beneath the mango trees, picking ripe fruit. Anansi climbed up into the balata tree and took his drum to distract Granny and make her dance. He opened his mouth and sang out as loud as he could. He let his voice soar above the treetops. He knew that she could not resist his music:

Aye yay, yay yay.
Dance, Granny, dance.
Aye yay, yay yay.
Lift up your foot and dance.

Anansi carried on playing, slamming his hands down onto the drum and singing aloud. Once again, Granny's shoulders started twitching and her toes started tapping. Before long, the Caribbean breeze drifted across, carried by the rhythm of the drum. It floated over to Granny and lifted her up. She danced and danced, twirling around across the fields. As soon as she was out of sight, Anansi scurried down from the tree and gathered up all of the ripe mangos she had picked, chuckling to himself at how clever he was.

'I could keep this up for days and we will never go hungry.' He was feeling very pleased and knew that his wife would not be able to scold him when he brought home another full basket of food. And he was right, she greeted him warmly and they all ate like kings and queens that night.

You might think that Anansi would feel guilty or a bit concerned about Granny by now, but he did not. He was only concerned with where his next meal was coming from. And so, before sunrise the next day he set out for Granny's field again. He clambered up into the same balata tree and waited for Granny to appear. It was so early that the cocks hadn't begun crowing. He lay back onto the branches, laughing and catching jokes with himself,

'Heh, heh. I wonder what free-ness I will get today.'

'He, heh, he. Eat little and live long.'

Anansi was so busy entertaining himself that he didn't notice Granny had crept out into the field. She knew that Anansi had been tricking her and she was ready for him today. Carrying her basket out to the starfruit trees, she muttered under her breath:

Fool me once Anansi, shame on you;
Fool me twice Anansi, shame on me!

As soon as Anansi saw her, he pulled out his drum and sang his tune. The rhythm took hold of Granny and she began to spin. She moved her waist and waved her arms, lifting up her foot to dance. But this time, when the Caribbean breeze drifted inwards, she stayed firmly in the field. She sashayed to the left and swooped to the right, holding her arms out in the air.

'The music sounds so good!' said Granny, dancing to the beat of the drums. Anansi looked on from the tree and saw her putting down some moves. He was expecting her to dance away but she didn't. As his hands slapped the drum skin, his own feet started twitching.

Granny's dancing was so delightful that he wanted to join in. His shoulders started bumping and his head started nodding.

Anansi felt the urge to go and dance. Granny leaped out from the trees singing:

> Aye yay, yay yay.
> Dance, Anansi, dance.
> Aye yay, yay yay.
> Lift up your foot and dance.

He jumped down from the tree and joined Granny in the field. Together they danced the night away, lifting up their feet and stamping down onto the soft earth.

It was true that Granny could not resist the music but she knew that Anansi could not resist the dance. And that night, Anansi danced all the way home, empty handed.

Patsy King, Jamaica

I was 5 years old when my mum left Jamaica to come to England without me. I wanted to come with her but she couldn't afford my passport at that time. The separation stayed with me for many years. My dad came to the UK after her but I stayed behind. I wanted to join them but the process of people's children coming to England was not so straightforward. I waited for another year before the paperwork was finally sorted out. I missed out on taking up a scholarship at a school in Clarendon.

I left Jamaica to come to England in 1965 when I was 14 years old. I travelled alone on the Italian ship Ascania *to Southampton, England. I was under the care of the ship's nurse as I was a minor. My uncle had given me a bag full of shillings. I was on the ship with lots of children who had taken two weeks to get to Jamaica from their islands. The* Ascania *then took another two weeks to get to England. I felt very grown-up travelling by myself. The nurse would take me to dinner with the captain and the ship's crew.*

When we arrived, it was dark and dismal, with lots of chimney smoke, like night spirits rising into the sky. That was my first impression of Southampton. It was the backs of the houses. It was so cold and looked horrible and dirty. It was not what I was expecting at all.

My dad collected me and took me to his house. He was a strict disciplinarian, he was a minister in the church. He had separated from my mum and remarried. He had a new family with children of his own. I looked a bit different from them and spoke very good English, so I didn't fit in very well. I hated everything.

There was no bathroom in the house. You had to go to the public baths to bathe with everyone else. In Jamaica, we had everything inside the house (unless you lived in the countryside). I kept asking my dad, 'When will you take me to see my mum?' She had left me at the age of 5 years old and I was yearning to see her.

After a few weeks, Dad drove me to meet my mum, who lived in Harlesden. She worked in the hospital as an auxiliary nurse. He gave me the option to go back with him and his new family or stay with my mum. She had a TV and she was a bit more lively (less strict than him) so I said I wanted to stay. I went to Haverstock Secondary Comprehensive School in Camden as my cousin went there.

I remember how bad the snow was. Piled up on the side of the pavement. It was bitterly cold. I had chilblains. My fingers would go green. I had just missed the awful fog of 1962 but it was still quite bad. Visibility was so limited that you had to walk in the middle of the road behind the bus to go to school, just so that you could see. I remember people talking about us (black people) as if we were filthy people from a faraway land. I thought, 'You've never even seen my land.'

At that time, people bathed their children in the kitchen sink and had their baths in the kitchen. They washed their dogs in the kitchen sink, the same sink where they brushed their teeth. It was such a shock to me, the way people lived here, and yet we were looked down upon.

There was lots of prejudice but there was also a sense of community in some areas back then. People would leave their back doors open, leave children in prams in the front yard to get fresh air and everyone would stop and chat to the babies. People looked out and helped one another, too.

I was interested in commerce at school but my mum registered me to be a nurse. I didn't want to do that because I was quite squeamish. The year before I left school I studied commerce. My tutor was impressed with me and I advanced quickly but when I left school I could not get a job. They said I had no experience. I just went to work as a clerk and did typing. My mum didn't have the money to help me further my education. There were lots of barriers to progression. Banks wouldn't lend black people money and we were held back more in that sense. We had to put aside our differences to try and get on. In order to save for our own house, we would pool our money together and 'throw a pardner'. We would take turns to get the lump sum. It was hard for a lot of us and a lot of us were in that position.

In a way, because of our years of separation across generations, it has affected us as a community and our ability to support each other and build upon that support. I believe it is crucial to maintain our stories and learn about our history. The stories are what unites us. My grandparents used to tell us stories of the Arawaks, the rebellious slaves who were taken to the island of Jamaica. We would fight to the death for our freedom. It was about survival and using your wits to get ahead. That instinct was still there when our parents came to England during the Windrush *years, too.*

Tony Liverpool, Dominica

Carpenter

My dad first came to the UK in 1956 (just after I was born). At that time my dad was an engineer and he worked in an engineering factory before working in Battersea Power Station. It was hard for him to make a decent wage and save. He put up with living with six people in a room while he worked here. A few years later, he sent for us to join him. We are a big family of three sets of families. There were eleven of us. We didn't all come together. My older brother and sister came first. I missed my siblings, it was not easy being separated from each other.

I came to England in 1964 when I was 8 years old. We travelled by the ship Ascania *and I remember it vividly. We embarked from Portsmouth in the north of Dominica and it was the first time I had been on such a huge locomotive. Everyone was hurrying around. It was noisy and quite exciting. I travelled with my sister and my mum. At that age it was an adventure for me.*

We came to live with my aunty at first. We rented two rooms upstairs in a house in Peckham on Montpelier Road. I didn't find school tough at all. It was different and not laid back but I got on OK. I did miss our home, our island. I have wonderful memories of us all living together in a big house. We would listen to my dad telling us stories. Sometimes they were scary stories to give us a warning or to share our ancestry. The West Indies is a very spiritual place and we carry that in our stories.

Trickster Tales

These stories are filled with humour and sometimes revenge. Remembering the social and historical context at the time these tales were passed down, the animal characters symbolise those in power or those who have nothing and seem weak but are clever enough to triumph in the end.

How Turtle Fooled Rat

Guyana

Once upon a very long time ago. Times were hard. When I say hard, I mean 'scrape the bottom of the rice pot' kind of hard. There had been a terrible drought across the islands and there was not enough food to go around. Everyone spent their days and nights searching for food. Everyone spent their days and nights talking about food. Have you ever noticed that even when you've just eaten, you start talking about what you'd like to eat for the next meal? Well, it was no different here. With little food to eat, everyone still talked about food: 'Wouldn't it be nice to have some sweet potatoes?' or, 'I could do with finding some ripe soursop.'

One blazing hot morning, Turtle was resting in the shade of a tamarind tree when Rat came strolling by. His fur was dull and his long tail dragged in the dirt. Turtle raised his tired head and they exchanged the usual pleasantries.

'How are things with you Turtle?' asked Rat.

'Oh, fine. Just fine. And you?'

'Couldn't be better,' replied Rat, hoping that his voice wasn't squeaking too high. It's probably fair to say that neither one of them would admit it if they weren't fine. In fact, Rat, who was a bit of a cunning fellow, began to boast about how the drought wasn't really bothering him.

'You know what Turtle, I can go for quite a while without eating', he said.

'Is that so?' Turtle looked thoughtful for a moment and then said, 'Why don't we see who can go without food for the longest?' For he was a creature who quite liked a challenge.

Rat's tummy was already concave and his skin was stretched tight, like a well-made drum, but he had no intention of refusing a challenge from Turtle.

'A competition? No problem,' said Rat. After all, he was a hardy bush rat, used to the rarity of food.

They agreed that they would pick a tree for each other and take turns to not eat any food until that tree bore fruit. Rat chose a plum tree and told Turtle to go first. He built a fence around the tree and Turtle made himself comfortable next to its slender trunk.

After a month, Rat came back to check on his friend. 'How are you doing Turtle?' He could barely hide the glee in his voice.

'I'm fine thank you.' Turtle's voice rang out loud and clear. After the second month, Rat felt sure that Turtle would be suffering. He strolled by the plum tree and greeted his friend. 'How are you doing Turtle? Still alive?'

Again Turtle replied quite cheerily. This performance carried on for several months. Rat would visit and poke his nose through

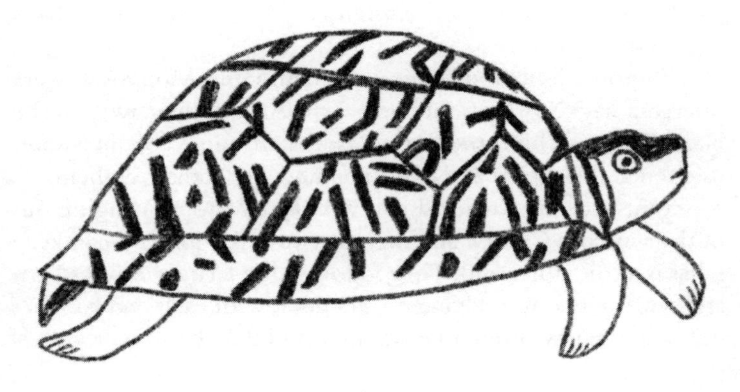

the fence that he'd built. He'd call out to Turtle, expecting to hear him begging for food, but Turtle was always chipper.

Soon the plum tree blossomed under the weight of the sun. The fruit hung down like sweet and sour diamonds, teasing him from above. Finally, an abundance of ripened fruit rained down onto the ground. Turtle ate until his belly was full.

Now it was Rat's turn and Turtle chose a cashew tree for him to sit under. He built a fence around its majestic trunk and told the bush rat to stay within its boundaries.

As before, one month went by and Turtle returned to check on Rat. 'How are you doing?'

'I'm doing OK,' replied Rat, trying to sound convincing. A second month went by and Turtle returned and called out again. 'How are you getting on my friend?' This time Rat's voice sounded a bit faint. 'Not bad. I'm a bit tired.'

After the third month, Turtle crawled up to the fence and shouted out to Rat. 'How are you now?' Silence. There was no reply. Turtle peered through the fence and saw Rat's dead body slumped under the tree. Rat did not know that the cashew tree only bears fruit once every three years.

Anansi and Mongoose

Jamaica

Once upon a long, long time ago, Anansi and Mongoose were offered a day's work on the local farm. After toiling away in the blazing hot sunshine, the farmer gave them some coconut water to quench their thirst and explained how he would pay them.

'Come into my barn and you will see two ropes hanging out of the window. Choose any rope that you like and you can keep what is at the other end.' They followed the farmer into his barn and saw the two ropes lying on the floor, with each end hanging out of a window. One rope was long and thin, but the other was thick and heavy. You can guess which rope Anansi wanted. He rushed up to the thick rope and declared, 'This one is mine! I got it first.' He grabbed it and began to imagine an abundance of riches at the other end.

Mongoose, being somewhat measured in his approach, picked up the thin rope and they both began to pull. The farmer shook his head and chuckled to himself in the corner of the barn.

'Eh-eh, this one has something big and juicy at the end,' said Anansi, struggling to pull the thick heavy rope. Mongoose took his time pulling the thin rope. He was just happy to be getting anything at all. What Anansi and Mongoose didn't know was that the farmer had tied a great big cow to the end of one rope and a tiny chicken to the end of the other rope.

As soon as Mongoose saw that he had a great big cow as his payment, he let out one long whistle. 'Wooooooooh. Look at this. What a surprise.' Anansi on the hand, was not pleased when his saw a tiny chicken on the end of his rope, but he didn't show it.

'Ooooh,' he sang, 'I'm going to have some nice roast fowl for dinner.'

Before parting ways, Anansi invited Mongoose to sleep over at his home for the night. 'You've been working hard all day Mongoose. Rest yourself tonight and travel tomorrow.'

It sounded like a good idea, and so the trusting Mongoose accepted crafty Anansi's offer. During the night, while Mongoose

slept, Anansi crept out to where the cow had been tied up in his yard. He cut off its tail and hid the cow in the bush behind his house. Then that crafty spider buried the tail in the ground, leaving only the bushy end sticking out of the earth.

The following morning, after a delicious breakfast of fresh eggs from Anansi's new chicken, Mongoose went to retrieve his cow. 'I'll be on my way now Anansi, thank you for breakfast.' he said. They strolled out to the front yard where Anansi started howling in horror. 'Oh noooooo! Look at your crosses Mongoose!'

He stood over the cow's tail, poking out from the ground. 'Your cow must have gone for a walk underground and now he's stuck.'

Anansi held his head in mock dismay and continued. 'Quick Mongoose, you better pull it out.'

Mongoose couldn't believe his eyes. He hurried over to the tail and tugged it out from the ground. It immediately popped out in his hand. He stood there, holding the cow's tail. 'Oh nooooooo!' cried Anansi even louder, 'Look what you've done Mongoose. You've lost your cow.'

Mongoose was stunned into silence. Anansi put his arm around his shoulders and offered some hope. 'Don't worry my friend, you can make some nice tail-soup from that.'

Poor Mongoose started to bawl. 'I don't want tail soup. I want my cow back.'

'I tell you what, let me help you out. Why don't you take my fowl and have it instead? I feel bad for you Mongoose.'

Mongoose refused to take Anansi's chicken. 'I don't want any chicken. I had my mouth set for some cow.' With his head hung low, he thanked Anansi for letting him stay and then headed off for his own home.

Once he was out of sight, Anansi did a little dance of victory, for now he had a cow and a chicken all to himself.

Jack Mandora, me no choose none.

Fowl & Hyena

Jamaica

One fine day, Fowl was cooking up his dinner deep in the middle of the forest. He was in a great mood. He began putting together a pile of twigs and shrubs, under the shade of a bayawon tree. He lit a fire and sang to himself, as ribbons of smoke danced above him through the leaves:

I have sweet potatoes and plantain, too
Mix with yam, I make nice fufu.

With a long stick, he poked and prodded the fire, turning over his sweet potatoes and plantains. 'Hm, almost done,' he thought. It was twilight and the forest was heaving with nightlife. The fireflies swarmed through the undergrowth, their bodies shimmering in the darkness. The tree frogs clung to branches and warmed up their voices, ready to croak out their night chorus, their bulging red eyes piercing the night.

In the distance was Hyena, panting, breathless and vex. He'd become separated from his pack and he was sure his friends were all feasting somewhere on the last hunt. The smell of the roasting sweet potatoes and ripe plantain weaved through the forest, past the giant tree ferns, right into Hyena's nostrils and down towards his empty belly.

He stepped lightly through the forest, following the sweet scent until he saw two large horns hovering above a fire. There was Brer Fowl, licking his lips and singing to himself:

I have sweet potatoes and plantain, too
Mix with yam, I make nice fufu.

'Evening.' Hyena's voice was tough, like nut brittle.

'Eh-eh,' Brer Fowl jumped back. He moved his neck from left to right and blinked through the flames. He couldn't see anyone beside him, but he knew that voice.

'Is that you Hyena?'

'I'm hungry.' Hyena stayed in the shadows.

'Well, I've got plenty of food, roast sweet potatoes, and plantains. You can share some with me,' he offered.

'I'm hungry. For fowl'.

Brer Fowl stepped back, his eyes darted through the trees, checking for an escape route. He knew he could never outrun Hyena.

'Listen, hold up a minute,' said Brer Fowl. 'Why don't you just let me finish my meal and then you can eat me? A full-bellied fowl is surely more appetising than an empty-bellied one.'

Hyena came forward and revealed himself. His black eyes carried death. His jaws were gaping wide as if he was about to laugh.

'Please Hyena, just let me just eat up my food quickly and then you can eat me.' Brer Fowl sounded so desperate that Hyena agreed. Fowl filled with sweet potatoes and plantains would make a nice meal indeed.

Brer Fowl pecked into the soft potatoes, taking his sweet time. He blew on the skin to cool them down. His beak moved slowly up and down while he swallowed loudly.

Hyena took a step forward, ready to pounce.

'Eh-eh. Take it easy Hyena. Give me a chance.' Brer Fowl's feathers were really ruffled now.

He began to peel off the charred skin from the yellow plantain. 'Are you sure you don't want any Hyena?' There's plenty for you too.

'Just hurry up Brer Fowl. I'm tired of waiting.' Hyena was already picturing making curry chicken when his sharp ears picked up the sound of a low, deep growl. He looked up and saw two amber eyes glinting through the grass. Black stripes across a face appeared next, then a body followed majestically.

'Eh-eh, Tiger. I am so glad to see you,' smiled Brer Fowl.

'Well, well, what is going on here? A hyena and a bird having dinner together?' Tiger circled the fire, keeping his eyes on them both. Brer Fowl mopped his brow and began explaining to Tiger that Hyena wanted to eat him. 'He won't even let me finish my meal first in peace.'

'Hmm, this is an interesting situation'. Tiger stretched out his front paws, letting his body drape heavily on the ground.

'Brer Fowl is right. Leave him to eat his food.' His words flew from his mouth like poison darts. Hyena sucked his teeth and snarled.

'Then,' drawled Tiger, 'you can eat him. And I can eat YOU.'

Suddenly the forest nightlife became silent. The monkeys stopped howling, the mosquitos stopped buzzing and even the rats stopped running. The sweet air that carried the scent of roasting food vanished.

'A hyena with a belly of fowl will make a delicious meal,' laughed Tiger.

Now, you may already know that a hyena is a pretty fast animal. They often run in packs and can catch large prey, but they aren't the most intelligent animals. In fact, it's fair to say that quick thinking is not in their skill set. Brer Fowl, on the other hand, had a swift mind. He nodded in agreement with Tiger and swallowed his last sweet potato.

'All that food has made me thirsty', declared Brer Fowl. 'Let me just catch a drink in that stream over there, to help my food go down.'

Tiger thought that sounded fine. Everyone knew that Brer Fowl was slow and feeble. Waddling on his two stick legs. Tiger kept his eyes fixed on Hyena while they both waited for Brer Fowl to return.

As soon as he was out of sight, Brer Fowl scrambled away as fast as his webbed feet could carry him. He ran this way and that way, twisting and turning, and soon had enough speed to flap his wings and fly. It was only about 10ft but it was high enough to get him away from those two cats.

Anansi, Tiger & the Magic Stools

Jamaica

In days gone by, Monkey was in charge of dealing out justice. No one knows how this came to be but here he was, holding court in a palace without walls or doors, sitting in judgement in the middle of the forest.

This was how the story goes. There were ten magic stools but nine of them were exactly the same. Each one about 2ft high and carved from the darkest mahogany trees. The tenth stool was the only one that was different. This stool was similar in size and shape but made of pure, solid, shiny gold. The wooden stools were positioned in a circle with the tenth golden stool in the middle.

Monkey and his chiefs of justice would swing from vine to vine, guarding the stools and listening to cases. Anyone accused of a crime would be brought in front of Monkey and asked to step on each magic stool, counting as they walked. If they were guilty of their crime, the magic stools would know. The accused would stand on the tenth golden stool and then instantly drop dead. That is how it went.

I'm going to tell you about the day when these judgements took a particularly nasty turn. Dog and Crab were lined up before Monkey. Each one was accused by Goat of stealing his yams. Lots of people turned out to see what would happen. These were the days when capital punishment was a bit of a sport. Lizard picked out a good spot on a tamarind tree, where he hung upside down. Rat brought his family of seven rats and they spread themselves out along the bushes. Monkey put on his special dark crimson robe, reserved for judgement days. He sat on a bamboo throne, chewing on a piece of sugar cane, and looked down upon Dog.

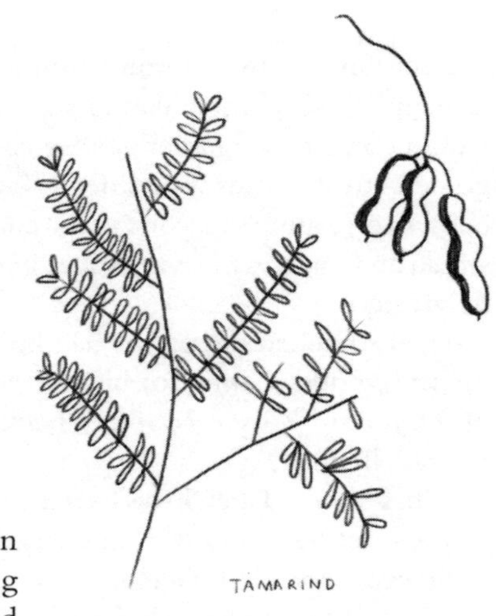

'You stand accused of stealing Goat's yams and sharing them with Crab. What do you say?' Dog scrunched up his face so that his black eyes were almost hidden by his long, black fur. His lip curled up in a snarl. He was vex and couldn't believe that he had to answer to Monkey.

'I didn't steal his damn yams. Goat is a liar!' barked Dog.

Monkey ordered him to count the magic stools and accept his fate. Dog stepped onto the first mahogany stool and yelled out 'ONE'. He continued until he got to nine and as he stepped onto the gold stool and yelled out 'TEN' he dropped down dead.

What a commotion that caused. Dog's family started wailing and crying. There was a lot of barking and growling too. They were upset and furious with no one to blame. While all of this was going on, no one realised that Tiger had been prowling around the edge of the court. His eye was bloodshot and his belly was empty. He needed a kill. Before Dog's family could take his body away, Tiger pounced. There was a flash of white teeth as his long body flew into the circle. He grabbed Dog by the neck and ran into the forest. There was such a commotion. Monkey was shrieking and yelling, his chiefs were jumping and climbing.

Everyone started running around and hiding. This continued to happen every single day. Tiger was on the rampage. Someone would come to judgement and as soon as they counted the tenth golden stool and dropped dead, Tiger would pounce from the bushes, terrorising everyone in the court. Monkey and his chiefs got scared and ran away, leaving Tiger in charge. This was exactly what he wanted.

Tiger stretched out on the bamboo throne, with his legs cocked up on the side waiting for his next victim. It was Crab. He sidled up expecting to see Monkey back, wanting to plead his case. Instead, he met Tiger.

'Oh, s-s sorry Tiger. I was looking for Monkey,' stammered Crab.

'He's not here now. I'm in charge.' Tiger licked his paws. A sly smile came across his face.

'Count the stools Crab. Let's see what happens'.

Crab tried to sidestep away but it was no use. Tiger roared at him: 'I SAID COUNT THE STOOLS.' Poor Crab had no choice. He climbed up and began counting and stepping. When he reached the tenth golden stool in the middle of the circle, he fell down dead. Tiger burst out laughing before picking him up and swallowing him whole, with one mighty, delicious crunch.

Well, you can imagine how panic had spread throughout the forest. All of the animals were talking about Tiger and how he had taken control. Once word got to our clever friend Anansi, he knew that he had to do something to get rid of Tiger.

He set out for the court, wracking his brains about what he could do, when he bumped into Wise Old Woman on the road.

'Are you heading to court Anansi?' she asked.

'Yes old woman, yes,' he nodded his head but carried on walking. 'I can't stop, I'm on serious business.' Anansi tried to hurry past, but Wise Old Woman wasn't finished yet. She carried a bag of herbs around her waist, which she tapped lightly.

'I think you'll need my help to beat Tiger,' she offered. Anansi was in no mood to chat, not even to Wise Old Woman.

'I'll speak to you later,' he said and pushed past her without even looking back.

'You'll regret this Anansi. I have plenty of spells. PLENTY,' she raged after him, shaking her stick in the air.

Anansi found Tiger strutting around the court like a newly appointed king. He had monkey's crimson robe draped over his long black stripes and all you could see were the tips of his white paws padding around the throne.

Without Tiger seeing him, Anansi climbed up into a banana tree and sat back comfortably peeling a banana, looking as if he'd been there all day.

Tiger looked up and saw him. He couldn't believe his audacity. 'ANANSI! What are you doing here?' bellowed Tiger. He didn't trust or like Anansi and knew he must be up to no good.

'I'm just thinking,' smiled Anansi, getting more comfortable in the tree.

'About what?'

'Oh,' said the trickster, 'I was just thinking how clever I am,' he grinned. Anansi knew exactly where to aim at Tiger's ego.

'If you're so clever Anansi, get down from that tree and count each one of these stools.' Tiger was pacing in circles below the tree, imagining Anansi in the grip of his teeth.

'OK, OK, but first you move away, I need a bit of space Tiger.' Anansi gathered his wits as Tiger backed away and then he stepped on to the first mahogany stool. He looked calm and not in the least bit worried.

This just annoyed Tiger even more. 'Hurry up and move!' ordered Tiger, so Anansi began to count as he stepped from one stool to the next.

'One, two, three, four, five, six, seven, eight'. Tiger's eyes narrowed as he watched him closely. He couldn't wait to pounce on Anansi's dead body.

'Nine …' Anansi suddenly stopped moving and said, 'and the last stool in the middle.' Tiger's mouth hung open in shock. He wasn't sure quite what happened but he knew that Anansi wasn't quite counting right.

'Count properly Anansi, do it again,' yelled Tiger.

'OK, OK, calm down. I don't see what the problem is, but if you insist,' he replied and went back to the first stool to start again.

'One, two, three, four, five, six, seven, eight, nine …' Anansi suddenly stopped moving and said, 'and the last stool in the middle.'

'NO. NOOOO!' roared Tiger. 'You are such a fool Anansi. That's not what you do. This is how you count.' Tiger shook off his robe, leaped onto the first stool and started to count as he stepped across each one. 'One, two three, four, five, six, seven, eight, nine, TEN.' As soon as Tiger stood on the tenth golden stool, he dropped down dead.

Anansi watched, his face beaming bright, with a broad smile. Then he noticed Wise Old Woman lurking in the bush. He wondered why she had come. What business could she have here?

He was just about to shoo her away when he Anansi noticed Tiger's huge body rise up from the floor. He stood up straight, very much alive and shook his head as if dazed.

Anansi leapt back in surprise, wondering if he was seeing things. It was very much Tiger but this time looking less brash and a little more sheepish. He checked his body over, turned and limped away into the forest.

Wise Old Woman let out a loud, deep laugh. 'You think you're so clever Anansi, but I told you, I have spells, plenty of spells,' she tapped her bag of herbs and disappeared into the forest. After that, the throne stayed empty. No one wanted to rule.

And that is how Tiger came back from the dead and why Monkey prefers to stay in the trees.

Nangato the Cat

Puerto Rico

Not that long ago, but far beyond here, there were families of mice scattered alongside the giant peak of Cerro de Punta on the mountainous island of Puerto Rico. Their village was north of the city of Ponce. The mice enjoyed a peaceful life, filled with an abundance of sunshine and tropical rains. They were surrounded by natural beauty with wild flowers, palm trees and crystal clear waterfalls. Their days were spent working on the land and their evenings stretched into the night with eating, singing and dancing.

Everyone looked out for each other, under the care and counsel of the *abuelita*, the grandma of the village. Her name was Maritza and she held meetings with the mice every Saturday night, listening to their worries, ideas and complaints. She would listen quietly to whoever came forward, nodding her head with encouragement or tutting with disapproval. She would offer her wise advice and respected opinion, making sure that arguments were resolved and harmony reigned.

At the end of these meetings, the mice cooked up a celebration of food for everyone to feast upon. Their little teeth chattered and their long tails swished as they danced and sang through the night.

On one of these balmy evenings, Santiago, an elderly mouse, shuffled over to Maritza and whispered in her ear. His face was ashen while he spoke and his words startled the *abuelita* so much that she covered her mouth in shock.

Everyone stopped what they were doing and wondered what could be so terrible that it could not be shared openly with their village. No one held secrets from each other and all business was aired for everyone to hear.

Maritza held her hand up to ask for attention. The mice all twitched with nervous fear. They gathered around and listened intently.

'My children, we have had some terrible news that will affect each and every one of us here.' Maritza paused and chose her words carefully. 'Santiago went down into the valley to visit his *prima hermana* [first cousin] and saw that a large black cat called Nangato had moved into the farm.

'A cat!' squealed some of the young mice.

'A large cat!' shrieked some of the older mice.

A flurry of commotion began with questions, panic and gruesome predictions.

'Tell us what you saw Santiago,' the mice cried out. They looked to their elder, who took centre stage ready to unfold the drama of how he uncovered the large, black cat. He began by explaining how he had been making one of his regular visits to his cousin's home. She makes the tastiest, fried tostones. He'd set off early in the morning, just after sunrise, and took the route past the flowing stream where you can look out across the mountain and see the whole of the island. He followed the winding path, which twisted and turned with the flow of the water. He moved swiftly across the main road, where traffic came flying from both directions. As he came towards the farm, he breathed in the familiar smell of fresh coffee from the fields. He was about to scamper over to the avocado trees, where his cousin lived, when he heard an unusual sound coming from under a bush. It was the low hum of a wheezing purr.

'I stopped in my tracks and looked about, knowing that something was wrong. My whiskers were twitching. I sniffed the air and saw my *prima hermana* hiding behind a rock. She looked terrified and beckoned me over, so I moved as swiftly as I could. I asked her what was wrong and she held her finger to her mouth. I stayed silent.' Santiago paused for effect, looking at all of the eyes watching and waiting for his next word.

'She pulled me towards the side of the house and we crouched down low. Together we peered through the long blades of grass and then I saw him!'

Loud gasps echoed around the mice. They all tried to picture what Santiago saw.

'What did he look like?' asked one mouse.

'Tell us. Tell us. What did you see?' pleaded another.

'Resting in between the scarlet petals of the hibiscus flowers, I saw the giant, black head of Nangato the cat. He was lying in the grass, licking his black fur. His long pink tongue was flying in and out of his huge mouth like this.' Santiago flicked his tongue out like a poisonous dart.

'Did he see you *tío* [uncle] Santiago?' his nephew wondered.

'No, he did not. I returned immediately to warn everyone.' Santiago finished his story to rounds of applause and congratulations for his bravery. *Abuelita* Martiza held up her hand again for quiet.

'Nangato the cat is a great risk to our village and our way of life. We will need to come up with a plan to keep us all safe from harm.' She opened the floor to ideas. No one said a word. Fear took over their mouths, stifling their voices into silence. Even Santiago did not have any ideas. He was worried that more cats may come prowling around the mountainside. Martiza decided that they had no other option but to befriend Nangato.

'If we reach out and offer him our hospitality, he will see that he does not need to harm us.' This idea was greeted with scepticism. Everyone trusted Martiza and they were used to letting her lead them in all matters of business but this seemed like a very risky idea and the cost of failure was high.

'I will go in person myself, to meet this Nangato,' she announced. Again this idea was met with doubt. No one wanted their beloved *abuelita* to put herself in danger but no one else was willing to go in her place. And so it was decided. Martiza would leave early the next morning and travel to the farm, where she would stand face-to-face with Nangato and offer the hand of friendship.

Just as darkness was leaving the island for the other side of the world, Martiza set off to find Nangato. She made her way nimbly down the mountainside, scampering over rocks and darting through grass. She walked nonstop all morning. By the middle of the day, the sun could be seen roasting from the sky like a ball of yellow flames. When it was at its most fierce, Martiza rested in the moss of a kapok tree before continuing on her way. It was a bright cloudless day and Martiza could see shades of blue scattered across the sky as she made her way along. She came over the hillside and saw Nangato lying down, dozing under a coconut tree. She stayed at the top of the hill and called out, '*Señor* Nangato! It is me, *Abuelita* Martiza.'

The cat lazily opened one eye and immediately spotted the mouse. So this is the famous *Señora* Martiza who everyone speaks of. He wondered if he could pounce upon her from where he lay. But she was standing at a safe distance and there was no way he could spring that quickly up the hill. Nangato stood up and greeted Martiza, asking what he could do for the little mouse.

'I have come to invite you to a fiesta in our village. We would like to be friends and live in peace with you, our neighbour.' Martiza spoke without fear, in a calm, confident voice. Nangato was suspicious at first and thought it could be a trap. Then he dismissed that idea. After all, what could a village of tiny mice do to him?

'Thank you for your delightful invitation,' Nangato purred. 'I would love to come. Expect me tomorrow, before the sun goes down.'

Martiza returned to her village and shared the news that the big, black cat was coming to party with them. The mice scurried around with excitement. There was much work to be done to prepare for the fiesta. They hung up colourful decorations of lanterns and streamers. '*Una fiesta*! *Una fiesta*!' They cried out aloud, stirring, frying and stewing their favourite foods. *Arroz y habichuelas* steeped in a pot with all the full flavours of rice and beans marinating with garlic, peppers and herbs. Plantain leaves were folded over stuffed green bananas to make *pasteles* and crescent-shaped *empanadas* were deep fried until crispy.

The next day, all the mice were ready and waiting for their guest to arrive. A trusted mouse was sent to fetch Nangato. He lay stretched out in the morning sun, dreaming about pouncing on all the mice in the middle of the fiesta, grabbing as many as he could to eat. He quickly rejected that idea. The mice were quick and could scatter into their hiding places, leaving him empty handed. He needed a better plan.

Carlos fetched Nangato and bravely brought him to their village. The mice were hushed into silence as the large, black cat strolled among them. His long tail black hung down with the white tip almost dragging on the ground. He moved slowly, letting his almond-shaped eyes drink in the scene. The mice crowded around him, cheering and stamping their little pink feet. Now the fiesta could begin. Nangato ate from their bowls and drank from their cups. He listened to their songs of brave mice exploring lands near and far.

Finally, late into the night he sank down on his white paws and closed his eyes for a sleep. The mice partied until dawn, overjoyed that they had made friends with their enemy. Mice drifted away to their homes to sleep, leaving Nangato right where he lay beneath the silver-lined leaves of a royal palm tree. It was not until later that morning that one of the mice took a twig and prodded him.

'Time to wake up Nangato. *La fiesta terminó*, the party is finished.' He tapped him several times on the head, but Nangato did not stir. He moved as close as he dared and peered at his face. Still Nangato did not stir.

'THE CAT IS DEAD!' Squealed the mouse. He scuttled around the village waking the other mice, calling 'Nangato, the big, black cat is dead.' Everyone crept out bleary-eyed from their homes to see for themselves. *Abuelita* Maritza examined Negato and agreed that he was indeed dead.

'We must bury him,' she declared. 'It is only right.' They all agreed. Feeling relieved that their enemy could no longer be a threat. Several mice set to work digging a hole in which to place his body, whilst others plaited leaves to make a stretcher. They sang while they worked, digging and stitching until everything was ready. It took many of the mice to lift Nangato's large body onto the stretcher. They covered him with flowers and stood in a circle while six of the strongest mice jumped into the grave. They stood down below, waiting to help lower the stretcher into the ground. They lowered the stretcher down slowly into the whole. They moved very carefully, as it inched deeper and deeper into the earth.

Once it touched the bottom, the six mice prepared to climb out when suddenly Nangato opened his eyes and sprang up from the stretcher. He pounced on the six mice as they scrambled and scurried to climb out of the grave. His claws ripped through them. Everyone screamed and shrieked with horror up above as they watched their friends getting eaten by Nangato. They begged and pleaded with him to stop but it was clear that he would not. There was nothing they could do but run into the mountains. Mice could be seen fleeing left and fleeing right. They escaped with their lives and hid between the rocks and the grass, deeply saddened by the loss of their friends. Nagato licked his paws and strolled back to his farm, fully sated and pleased with himself.

And that is why to this very day, mice will never trust a sleeping cat again.

Anansi & Fire

Jamaica

Fire was one of those girls that everybody wanted to be around. She was bright, confident, and exciting. Anytime Fire was there she was the centre of attention. She just had a hypnotic way about her. In the evening people sat around her telling stories way into the night. In the tropics, crickets chirped, fireflies lit up the grass like twinkling fairy lights and Fire comforted everyone with the heat of her flames.

If there was a dance going on, Fire was there, dazzling in red and yellow. She'd put down the best dance moves, flickering to the left, swaying to the right, her flames reached up high into the sky. Everybody thought she was hot, especially Anansi and he was a single man at this time. He'd had his eyes on Fire for a long time.

He kept trying to think of ways that he could catch her, tame her and keep her for himself. If any of you have known someone like Fire, you know they cannot be contained. They need their space. But Anansi liked a challenge and so one day he headed into the bush. He passed his friend Rat, who was quite a distinguished-looking fellow. One of those guys who is always dressed up smart. He considered himself quite dapper and always had a shiny new coat and a crisp-looking haircut.

'Where are you off to in such a hurry Anansi?' asked Rat.

'I'm going to try my luck with Fire tonight.' Anansi puffed up his tiny chest. 'The last time we chatted, there was definitely a spark between us.'

Rat let out one big booming laugh. 'You'll need more than luck, Anansi. She's way too hot for you!' He scurried off laughing, leaving Anansi a bit aggravated. There was no love lost between those two. Regardless, Anansi carried on and he soon found Fire sleeping under the flame tree. Some people call this tree the flamboyant tree in the Caribbean. It has beautiful bright red flowers that fan out around its branches. Here was Fire, small and

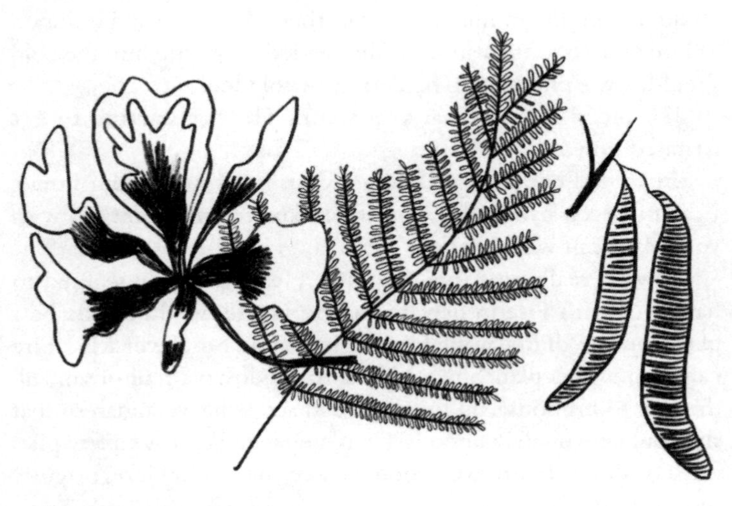

FLAMBOYANT TREE

flickering at the root of the flame tree. She flared up instantly when she saw Anansi.

'My, my, Anansi. How nice of you to come and see me,' she giggled, all bright and luminous. She'd been feeling lonely lately and really wanted some company. Anansi didn't step too close but even from a distance, he could ooze charm.

'Look at you Miss Fire! You are so pretty!'

She giggled some more. 'You think so Anansi? You wouldn't lie to me now, would you?'

Anansi put on his serious face, well the most serious he could conjure up. 'Would I lie to you Miss Fire? Never!'

He stepped a bit closer. 'Why, I was just telling my good friend Rat how I would like to spend some time with you.'

Fire was getting really excited now. She encircled him with her flames. Anansi stood in the centre completely engulfed by fire.

'Hold on a minute, slow down. I don't want to get burned,' shrieked Anansi. Fire lowered herself and calmed down. 'How are we going to spend any time together Anansi?' she pouted and turned her back on him.

The trickster racked his brains and said coyly, 'Why don't we climb up into the mountainside together where we can be alone?'

Fire refused to turn around. She carried on giving him the cold shoulder, with her flames flickering a cool blue.

'Tell me what is it that you want?' He was starting to get irritated now.

She folded her arms and said, 'I want to come to your house. I can't be seen hanging out on street corners or mountains with you. My mum will get angry.'

Now he really was in a dilemma. He desperately wanted to hang out with Fire in private and his house would be the best place, but he didn't want Fire to destroy it. So clever Miss Fire came up with a plan. She told him to lay down a trail of sand all the way to his house, up the steps, and across his verandah so that she could burn safely upon it. Then he needed to leave a few piles of rubbish inside his front room where she could blaze, brightly just for him.

This sounded like a good plan. Anansi rushed home and swept from top to bottom. He made everything nice and clean. He even gave the front of his wooden house a new lick of paint. It was a burning bright yellow. Just as she'd instructed, he laid a trail of sand all the way through the village, up to his front steps and across his veranda. He collected twigs and rubbish and made a nice pile in his front room. Finally, he was ready for his date with Fire.

Later that night when the sea breeze blew in from the east, Fire came flickering through the forest. She picked up speed along the sandy trail, snaking around the towering lime trees and thick mango groves. The breeze blew into Fire, carrying the smell of frying fish and pumpkin stew from the kitchens she passed along the way in the village.

Fire was growing in size and strength. When she finally reached the steps of Anansi's wooden house built high up on stilts, she was now a raging, roaring fire. He was in the front room waiting to greet her, adding the finishing touches to his pile of leaves and by the time he saw her brilliant glow on the verandah, it was far too late. Fire burst through the door and lit up Anansi's entire house with flames. He leapt out of the way and dashed out through the back door, leaving her inside to blaze.

'How is this Anansi? Am I hot enough for you now?' she called out mischievously, her flames rising to the roof. Anansi watched, stunned as his home was completely burned down by Fire.

And that, everyone, is why no one in the Caribbean lights a fire in their house to this day.

ROSAMUND GRANT, GUYANA

Author, Mother and Grandmother

I came to England when I was 15 years old to join my mother, who had come to the UK a few months before to further her career in teaching. My father had recently been attending Reading University, studying for an additional teaching diploma before returning to Guyana. I flew out on British Overseas Airways Corporation (BOAC) accompanied by a family friend and was met by my mother at Gatwick Airport. It felt like an adventure – quite exciting, but bittersweet.

I was excited to join my mother because I had missed her, but I was also quite sad because I was leaving my childhood friends, father and siblings in Guyana. I was not meant to join my mother for another year, but my father brought forward my departure because he was worried about 'keeping an eye on a teenage daughter' over the school summer vacation while he was working. He had noticed that the local boys were taking a keen interest in me!

From attending convent kindergarten through to convent high school, my friendships had been well-established. My school, St Joseph's Catholic Girls, was relocating to a picturesque spacious area by Georgetown sea coast. There were to be new beginnings that summer without me! I don't think my parents thought it would affect me that much, they didn't worry about those aspects. It wasn't something that was considered in those days – in the face of a new life in the UK, offering better education opportunities for our family. Many professional Guyanese people came to the UK in the 1960s to further educate their children, because the University of Guyana had not yet been established.

My parents were both educators. Mum was known as a gifted teacher, who had a way with underachievers, and dad was a head teacher. My siblings and I were sent to the top schools and you were expected to obtain good grades, achieve and be successful in your chosen career. My brilliant older brother had received a Guyana scholarship to attend the University of the West Indies in Jamaica, as he wanted to be a physicist. My younger brother was still at St Stanislaus, a Jesuit college in Guyana, when I came to England. My two younger sisters were both still in primary school.

Arriving in London was a bit of a shock. Why had we come to a place that was so cold and grubby, with lots of factories? I remember when we were coming on the train from Gatwick seeing smoking chimneys, joined-up unpainted houses and lots of washing lines. I didn't realise that was the backs of the houses and I was not at all impressed!

My mum could not get a teaching post when she came because the British would not accept her teaching qualifications, so she had to retrain for two years. To make ends meet, she found a job in a paper doily factory – stencilling and then 'bashing' doilies to remove the unwanted bits. She just took it all in her stride. She was elected shop steward representing and supporting mainly white working-class women, by trying to improve their conditions on the shop floor. She also was in demand to help the children of migrants from the islands with reading and English.

We lived in a large rundown tenement house off the Old Kent Road. It was horrible, with flakes of paint falling from the kitchen ceiling. Mum said it was 'just for now' as they were saving for my sisters' fares to the UK. Things would get better and they did. We moved to our cousin's house in Herne Hill, as she rented two rooms. It was a beautiful, large, detached house in a leafy street and not too far from her work and Brixton, where my mother did the shopping.

I had enrolled in Peckham Girls' there and I was the only black girl in my class. The girls used to laugh at my 'quaint' ways and accent. Respect for teachers was paramount in Guyana – so if a teacher spoke to me, I would stand up and reply politely. The other pupils did not, because it wasn't part of their culture – so they called me good goody, but we became friends and they taught me how to speak 'Cockney' – much to my mother's dismay! I was quite bright at school and streets ahead of my peers in maths and English, as Guyana had one of the highest literacy levels in the Caribbean in those days.

My family then moved to a three-bedroom flat in a house in Hornsey, because my brother Bernie joined us within a year of my sisters. Although our arrivals were staggered, there was no huge gap between us all coming together as a family. My mother retrained and eventually taught at a school in Haringey for many years.

When we came to England, we met black people from all over the world – you met Africans, Jamaicans and other islands. What was brilliant is that we had to let go of all those prejudices we had inherited from colonisation and the 'divide and rule' system. It didn't matter which island people came from in the Caribbean – we united as a black community – through sharing food and cultural events. For example, joining a partner or boxhand. This was a system of pooling savings together for buying houses etc.

Growing up in London, I did not experience overt racism in the same way as a lot of other black people, it was more subtle. As a young adult, at times it was more blatant – especially in some of my professional training institutions. I qualified as a psychoanalytic psychotherapist and in my practice witnessed the impact of racism and discrimination; displacement, loss and separation on the mental health and lives of so many of us. In my opinion, it continues to ricochet through the generations to the present day.

By the way, there is another side to me – I am a published author of four cookery books in the UK and passionate about exploring food and food culture.

I'm very interested in my ancestry and went to Ghana for a while – visited the Elmina Slave Castle and Port. My mother used to tell us about our ancestors who were enslaved in Guyana – the Coromantee people from Ghana. When my brother Bernie (MP for Tottenham) died, I was asked to do some research into our ancestry for a BBC documentary presented by Kurt Barling and I found out that the Blairs (my mum's maiden name), were from the Blairmont Sugar estate in Berbice, Guyana.

On my father's side, my great grandmother was from Sierra Leone. She came to the islands long after the slavery, to work as a servant. My father also spoke of the three brothers enslaved on the 'Grant Plantation'. Therefore, they bore the name Grant. They were dispersed in the islands, but one brother came to Guyana – so the story goes.

We were told lots of stories about Africa at school by the nuns and priest who taught us – but nothing positive. We've had to let go of such lies and negativity to become a community. We have a shared history and ancestry. We embrace our differences, diversity and relish our connectedness. It is paramount to tell our stories and folklore to remind ourselves and teach the younger generations that we have more than survived – we have turned it around and, to quote Maya Angelou: 'and still I rise' – and Still We Rise.

Barbara Garel, Jamaica

Auxiliary Nurse, Mother of Six, Grandmother and Great-Great Grandmother

My husband first came to England with his brothers and sisters and so I came to join him here. He was here for five years before I joined him. That's how it was then. Usually the men came first and the wives followed, sometimes with or without their children. Hardly a complete family migrated together. We were all separated for many years. Once I was here, I looked after the children while he worked. Only one of you could work because child care was very difficult.

My first impression of London was terrifying. The smog was frightening to me and something I wasn't used to. We lived in Edmonton and I would leave our house and get lost. I couldn't find my way back home even if I asked people for help. Everything was wet and dark with the smog and the streets and bus routes were unfamiliar to me.

Eventually we moved to Doncaster and I preferred it to London because it wasn't as busy. I never got lost and people were more friendly. Our neighbours were wonderful. We had great neighbours and we looked out for one another. We babysat for each other and the children played together in the parks. I had two children then and became an auxiliary nurse. School was difficult for our children. The teachers were not very nice to them and they were unhappy in school until they reached secondary school and things were different. They were treated more fairly.

I'm from Kingston in Jamaica and I remember growing up listening and telling stories all the time. There were twelve of us in my family and we'd gather together early in the mornings and in the evenings on the veranda. We'd listen to my gran telling us stories. It was wonderful.

Love & Loss

These stories are a mixture of legends and folk tales, set in real places, telling about the lives of the indigenous people from the Caribbean islands and their spiritual beliefs.

The Legend of the Giant Water Lily

Guyana

Far back in the mists of time when the world was very young, the Caribs were the first people who lived in Guyana. Their homes of thatched palm leaves were scattered around the rivers and creeks. These were the water people who carved long canoes from the trunks of trees to sail down the great Amazon River.

Most evenings, after a feast of roasted fish and pounded cassava with beans, the elders would tell stories to the villagers. They'd gather under the giant silk cotton tree, said to be the keeper of the spirits, and tell tales of their ancestors and of fierce battles between the Caribs and the Arawâks.

One such night, the girls huddled together in the darkness. Their long dark hair hung like cloaks around their backs with their skin bronzed like cinnamon trees. The youngest of their group was called Balandra and she looked up longingly at the sky, letting the stories of Tamosi, their ancient sky god, carry her away. It was a well-known belief among the Carib people that the beauty and power of the universe would transfer on to anyone who could reach any part of its nature.

'Oh, how I wish we could touch the moon,' said Balandra. She stood up on her toes and stretched her arms out to the sky. She looked up into the stars, picturing the magical myth of the first Caribs who dwelt on the shimmering moon before they descended to the dark earth. The story had enchanted her so much that she desperately wanted to seek out the beauty and power held within the night sky. The next evening, she looked longingly at the moon and then an idea came to her.

'If I climb to the top of this tree, I will be closer to the night sky and our god Tamosi. I could then reach out and touch the moon.' She imagined a shower of glistening light rays falling upon her if she could touch the stars.

Without waiting for her friends, she climbed fearlessly up the trunk of the tree, stepping on the branches and pulling on its vines. The tree frogs croaked and the crickets chirped, as if to spur her on. She reached out from the highest branch but still could not touch the moon. Her fingers grasped the humid, night air. 'I will not give up,' she said, her voice rising above the canopy of leaves.

The following evening everyone gathered around the slender Mora to listen to the story of Oko-yumo, the water spirit with a human head and long, coiling body of a giant anaconda. Drummers tapped on their drums, guiding the rhythm of the story. Some of the girls began to dance, pounding the earth with their bare feet in time to the drums as the story was being told.

'Oko-yumo lay waiting for her victim in Wakapoa Creek. He had been warned not to seek her out. But he did not listen. She rose from the black water with her long, heavy tail and seized his body,' said the storyteller.

The drummers changed tempo and the dancers moved faster, swinging their arms through the air like bats hovering at night. The story continued.

'He could not scream out. His bones all shattered as Oko-yumo the water spirit coiled her tail around him and squeezed tightly.

Balandra was only half listening. Her mind was still on how to reach the moon. When one of the group suggested a night walk up through the mountains. she came up with another idea. 'Follow me up to the Roraima mountain peak,' she said. 'From there we can gaze in wonder at the night sky and reach out to finally grasp the moon,' she said, breathless with excitement. They all knew of her passion to touch the moon and agreed to make a late-night climb.

With the sky lit up by the stars above, Balandra led her friends to the highest mountain. They walked through vibrant valleys and across sandy marshes. They clambered over sandstone rocks and glided through low-hanging mist. The air tasted fresh as they walked higher and higher. The sprinkling rain kept them cool, gently tapping them on their heads and shoulders. They climbed through the night until they finally reached the peak of the mountain. There, they all stood, sinking into the darkness, and called out, 'Tamosi hear us now! Grant us permission to touch the moon and the night stars.' They stretched their arms out to the night sky, but the great sky god did not answer. They were disappointed again when they could not touch the moon.

The following night, when they had finished telling their stories and songs, Balandra took one of their dugout canoes and sailed down the river. She was restless and unwilling to give up her hope of touching the moon. The air was damp with heat and she lowered her hands into the river while floating aimlessly along. Just ahead of her, she noticed the moon, luminous and rippling in the clear water.

At last, she thought. I can reach out and touch it.

Without a moment's hesitation, she dived into the water, breaking through the reflection of the moon. She pushed herself down and sank deep into the river, twisting through giant reeds and moss. Her eyes peered out into the cloudy water, searching for the bright face of the moon.

'It was here. I just saw it,' she thought, looking around in frustration.

Her breath started to run out but she was too determined to find what had almost been in reach. Struggling for breath, she carried on swimming downwards, deeper and deeper towards the river bed. She grabbed at the reeds and pulled herself down further, desperately looking for it. But she found nothing and was soon out of breath. She was trapped down below and could not reach the surface in time to gasp for air.

Above the surface, the water became still. The reflection of the moon returned and there was no sign of Balandra. She had sunk to the bottom of the river. Her life ebbed away before she could return to the surface.

The supreme water goddess of rivers, lakes and seas – Atabey, looked down from the sky and took pity on this young girl. She decided to save Balandra and immortalise her. Sending a stream of glowing green light that swirled beneath the water, Balandra's lifeless body slowly transformed into a dark green, graceful water lily. She became a large flower with layers of petals that cradled each other. When the sun rose into the sky, each petal changed colour from white to pink with each passing hour. The lily slowly stretched out and blossomed over the day.

Balandra is known to this very day as the Victoria Amazonica – the largest water lily in the world with the most potent, heady scent.

When you next visit Guyana, look out for these beautiful giant water lilies gliding along the rivers.

The Fairymaid's Lover

Trinidad

There once was a time when you could catch a glimpse of the merfolk who dwelt in the wine-dark rivers and cobalt blue seas surrounding the Caribbean islands of Trinidad and Tobago. They'd leave a sparkling ripple in the water once their bodies had dipped below the surface. Or they sent the white-capped waves crashing into rocks after their tails had lashed the sea. These merfolk are the male mermaids. They are said to have upper bodies that resemble ancient warriors and kings, with unyielding faces and broad torsos. Their lower bodies resemble fishes with mighty tails thrashing in the sea. The fairymaids are the females of the species who lurk in waterfall caves, in rivers beneath bridges and beside water wheels. Don't be fooled by their alluring faces, long dark hair and iridescent tails. They are water spirits with the power to poison your mind and lure you to your death if their search for human love is unrequited.

This is what they say happened to Johnny Ryan many years ago. He was a fisherman by trade and most men were in his sleepy village near the Caroni River. There were plenty of kingfish and tarpon to catch in the ocean. Yet Johnny found himself drawn to the river, a river that snaked lazily for over 25 miles across the island. Perhaps it was the sweet smell of the pomerac trees that tempted him, with its crimson fruit that hung like jewels waiting to be snatched. Or maybe it was the solitude of the forest that drew him in. Whatever it was, Johnny would wade out into the river and cast his blue net. It was not long before he was rewarded with a haul of giant-sized fish. Their lustrous bodies glowed in his net like an undiscovered treasure. He staggered and strained with the weight of his catch as these magnificent creatures wriggled and flapped trying to get free. Johnny had never seen such large fish before. They were half the length of his body and had such a dazzling array of colours.

He returned the next day and the same thing happened, only this time he saw a mighty tail twist free and dart away from his

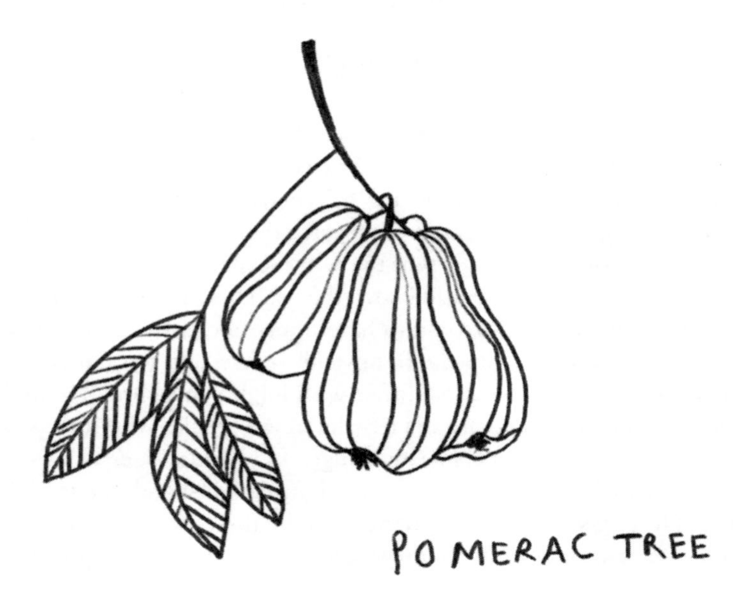

net. It was a fairymaid, who had been watching him from below. She swam too close to the surface, trying to protect the river fish and was nearly caught herself. Under the dazzling gaze of the sun and the sweltering humid heat, Johnny wondered if his eyes were deceiving him. He felt sure that he'd seen a woman in the water.

That night, with his window slightly ajar for the sea breeze to drift in, he tossed and turned in his bed. His sleep was filled with visions of a fairymaid calling him to the river. Her face was hidden in his dream, a dark hollow surrounded by tumbling black tresses. She sang a verse that pierced his heart with longing:

Come to me Johnny, come down to the river.
Catch me if you can.

He woke up in a cold sweat and made his way under the cloak of darkness, back to the river where he usually fished. He felt haunted by his dream. As he stumbled through the forest, he heard a mournful voice, singing through the trees. It was the voice from his dream, drawing him closer, whispering an eerie melody of lost love and times gone by.

He pushed back the bushes and saw a creature sitting on the river bank. She had the body of a woman but from the waist down the tail of a fish. Her dark skin was partly hidden by tresses of thick black hair, which she sat combing while she sang. Her long, heavy tail was covered in lustrous scales stretched out across the rocks. As soon as she heard Johnny behind her, she dived back into the water.

'Don't go,' he called out, stretching his arms out across the water. 'Tell me your name.' She circled beneath the surface and slowly let her head rise above the water, revealing the darkest eyes that appeared to stare right through his soul.

'I saw you in my dreams,' he said. 'I felt you calling me.' He was close to the water's edge now, trying to get near without wading in. The fairymaid pulled herself up to the rocks and allowed Johnny to come close to her. He drank in her long gaze and she beckoned him to embrace her. She clung to him, whispering words he could not understand, all night long, until the golden edge of the sun peeked out across the horizon.

The next few days found Johnny drifting along in a blurry haze. He was consumed with desire. He stopped doing repairs to his house, stopped fishing in the river and never turned up to domino nights with his friends. His sleep was haunted with dreams of the fairymaid calling him to her in song. He wandered around the streets at dawn, in a delirious state, muttering and humming to himself.

It wasn't until the villagers were attending the wake of old man Williams that Johnny was seen by his friends. He did not really want to be there as he had never liked old man Williams, but he decided to pay his respects to the grieving family.

He sat on the steps of their verandah while visitors came with offerings of pholourie fritters, coconut bakes and pelau rice. Neither the enticing smell of spices nor the loud cries of wailing people moved him. He sat glumly in a corner until his friend Big Toby spotted him.

'What's happened to you Johnny? We're not seeing you these days. You win some big money?' Johnny was relieved to speak to Big Toby, who only got that name because he barely reached 5ft tall. When Johnny poured out his heart about the fairymaid, Big Toby let out one long whistle.

'Oooooooooooh. You are bewitched my boy. The fairymaid has set her sights on you. We need to get you some help before it's too late.' He was referring to Ma Hilda, the wise old woman in the next village. She was versed in all the ways of the spirits and could advise them on how to help Johnny. They visited her the next day in her small hut, deep in the forest. She shook her head, letting the beads dangle around her neck.

'Your friend's shadow is slowly fading away,' she said. 'The fairymaid wants his spirit and if she gets it, he will be lost to her forever.'

Big Toby did not like the sound of that. 'What should we do Ma Hilda?' She advised them that the only way for Johnny to rid himself of the fairymaid's hold was to go to the water after midnight and plead for her to release him.

'Take a spare pair of shoes with you. Take off one pair and set fire to it right there on the river bank. Let it burn to ashes. When she reveals herself in the water, she will ask for payment for her unrequited love. Tell her 'only one pair of shoes'. Then take off your other pair of shoes at the water's edge. Turn them upside down and walk away, never turning back to face her.'

These days, that might seem like superstitious nonsense, but to Big Toby and Johnny it was old-time wisdom and beliefs. Both men agreed that Big Toby should accompany Johnny to the river that night, to encourage him to break the spell the fairymaid had over him. With their path faintly lit by the moon, they walked through the forest to the bend in the river where Johnny first met her. His friend hid in the bush while Johnny waited at the water's edge.

Before long, she swam to the surface and glided over towards Johnny. Floating in the water among a cluster of stars reflected from the sky, she appeared illuminated. Her dark skin glowed with a silvery outline and she beckoned Johnny to come to her in the river. He hesitated, feeling torn with love and confusion, when Toby's voice abruptly hissed from the trees, 'Ask her to release you, man. Hurry up.'

He was worried that Johnny's shadow was disappearing, along with his strength to resist the fairymaid. He knew all too well that once Johnny entered the river, that would be the last he saw of him. Somehow, Big Toby's voice jolted Johnny out of his reverie. He placed the spare pair of shoes on the ground and set fire to them. As they burnt to ashes he pleaded with the fairymaid. 'Please release me from your hold.'

Her face, once serene and charming, now twisted into a grotesque scowl to reveal rows of sharply pointed teeth. 'What is my payment?' she hissed.

Johnny was overwhelmed by her reaction. He stuttered and no words came out. Toby ran out from his hiding place, grabbed Johnny's arm and pulled him in the direction of home. The fairymaid shrieked a high-pitched squeal, which pierced the night sky and shattered their ears. She uttered a fowl curse to Johnny, which flew through the forest and grabbed him by the throat:

Bring yourself to me
Your shadow is mine
I gon' catch you here, you'll see in time
Bring yourself to me
I demand my pay
If I can't have you,
You'll die this day.

Johnny ran through the forest with Big Toby leading him as fast as he could, away from the river. They never looked back but he had not offered the payment of shoes. The fairymaid's curse struck terror into Johnny's heart. Safely back home, he hoped that would be the end of it.

'You must NEVER go back to the river,' said Big Toby, huffing and puffing, trying to catch his breath. 'The only thing you can do is stay away from there and keep your distance.' He hoped that his friend would heed his advice.

It was a restless night for Johnny. With the curse now upon him and his shadow almost gone, he didn't know what to do. While he slept, the fairymaid visited him again in his dreams. Her face was etched in mercurial charm as she showed him piles of golden coins in a large chest at the bottom of the river. Her chilling voice called him to come and find the buried treasure. He dreamt of the large chest full of gold coins.

Johnny awoke from the dream and felt uneasy. He looked under his covers and was startled to see three gold coins in his bed. He picked them up and bit them. They felt hard and definitely real. He leapt up from the bed in excitement. This must surely be a message from his fairymaid. He felt that the dream must be true. She wanted to lead him to untold riches.

He told no one of his dreams, not even Big Toby, and made his way back to the river during the day. He foolishly thought that he would be fine in the daytime, as he used to be when he first fished in the river. He waded into the murky waters with a shovel and his net. He moved across towards the other river bank where the tall reeds grew and dipped his head into the water. To his delight he saw shoals of shimmering fish scurrying away and a pool of light at the bottom of the river bed. Johnny felt sure this was where the treasure lay. There in the middle of the day, with only the cuckoo birds and coconut trees to witness, Johnny dived down into the river.

Some say that the fairymaid grasped him tightly and never let go, transforming him into one of the male mermaids that dwell in those muddy waters. Others say that he met his death searching for buried treasure. I say that we will never know what happened to Johnny Ryan, except that he was never seen again.

The Poisoned Roti

Trinidad

On the islands of Trinidad and Tobago, there was a young girl named Beatrice who accidentally murdered her brother. It all began soon after he left their family home to seek his fame and fortune. The house was bereft after he'd gone. Everyone missed seeing his shining face, with bright almond-shaped eyes and cheeks, which were forever filled with a smile. They missed the tapping of his light feet, which seemed to dance when others walked, and the melody of his deep voice when he sang. Most of all, they missed the soulful songs he strummed on his guitar in the evenings. They used to sit outside under the stars, chatting, singing and dancing in time to his tunes. He'd slap the barely polished wood to keep time, flick his fingers over the frets and they'd all cry out for more. Once he was gone, Beatrice ached for his presence. The house felt dark and empty. Somehow the sun seemed to shine brighter when he was there.

One day, their mother was cooking roti in the kitchen at the back of their house. She hummed songs that reminded her of her son, and she kneaded dough into a large ball before leaving it to rise. When she returned it was swollen and ready for her to roll

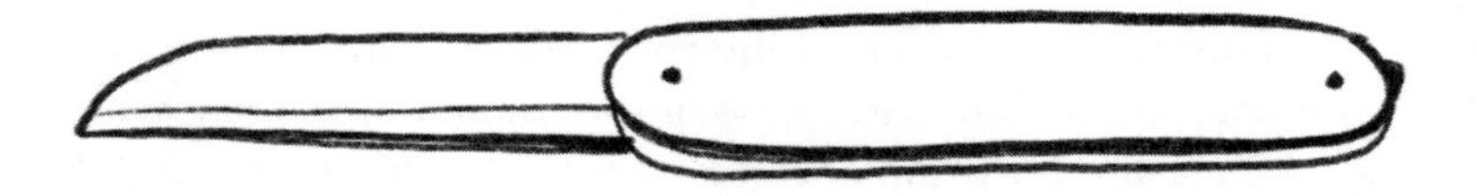

into small pancakes, which she fried on the roti pan. Soon there was a stack of fresh rotis piling up high on the window sill, waiting to be eaten with a bowl of hot curry and rice.

It was usually about this time of day that Bo would shuffle by. He was an elderly man who wore or carried all that he owned: an orange shirt that had lost its shine, baggy grey shorts with deep pockets, a penknife, a rucksack with a threadbare blanket given to him by the local pastor, two ripe mangoes he'd snatched from the neighbour's tree and a hollow giro that he played whenever he could find a stick to run up and down its ridges. With no fixed address or money to speak of, he relied on the generosity of others. He followed the smell of fresh pastry and stood at their kitchen window.

'Afternoon Ma King,' greeted Bo, revealing a head full of missing teeth.

'Afternoon Bo,' said Beatrice's mother, smiling to herself, for she knew exactly what was coming next.

'Any spare roti for me on this beautiful day?' he asked politely, his eyes boring sharp holes into the stack of pasty.

'Why of course, Bo, let me wrap some up for you. Careful now, they're too hot to eat straight away.' She handed him the food and waved him on his way. Beatrice stood in the doorway with her hands folded across her chest. Her dark eyes rolled to the heavens and her nose wrinkled up in disgust.

'Why do you feed that old man? You're encouraging him to beg.' she fumed. Her face turned bitter, like sour cherries.

'God doesn't like ugly, my child,' replied her mother without looking up. She carried on flipping rotis on the pan. Beatrice hated seeing Bo hanging outside of their house each day. She hated that he never said thank you and she hated the attention her mother gave to him. Of course, she was really just angry at her brother for leaving her behind. Beatrice stomped outside and watched as Bo walked past the front of their house. She stared at his dark brown feet, which were dry and cracked at the heels. She saw him tuck the rotis into his deep pocket. Her mind churned over ways to stop him from coming by their house every day. He looked up and caught her hard glare. He felt her rage leap out and stab him with murderous thoughts.

'Child, the good you do comes back to you. The evil you do stays with you,' he warned and nodded goodbye before strolling into the forest. This only made her more angry. How dare he counsel her. She was 13 years old. Almost a woman, she thought.

The next day Beatrice accompanied her mother in the kitchen and offered to help prepare the rotis. Mother and daughter hummed and chatted together, mixing flour and water, sprinkling a little salt to make their dough. Beatrice watched as her mother set aside the first few cooked rotis for Bo and, when her back was turned, she sprinkled rat poison over them. Just enough to make him a bit ill, she thought.

Later that day, Bo shuffled by the kitchen window as usual. Mother was flipping rotis on the pan.

'Afternoon Ma King,' he sang. 'How are you today?'

'I'm doing fine, Bo. Would you like some roti?' she asked, handing him the rotis she'd set aside, not waiting for the reply.

'You know exactly what I need.' He smiled, took the hot package and stuffed it into his pocket. 'I'll eat it later.' They exchanged pleasantries while Beatrice looked on, puzzled as to why he wouldn't eat it straight away. She rushed over to the window. 'The rotis are best eaten when they are hot,' she ordered, putting herself between him and her mother. Bo nodded in reply and shuffled away.

He headed into the forest to find somewhere to rest for the evening. It was late afternoon with only a few more hours of sunlight left. He walked slowly through the dense, dark woods, following a path that led out of the village.

The air was humid and dripping with heat, making Bo feel quite tired. He nestled down to rest at the trunk of a gnarly tree when he heard singing in the distance. A young man came into view, hacking at the bush with a machete. His skin, the colour of burn orange, was dripping with sweat, which pooled around a shirt tied at his waist. His guitar was slung over his shoulder and he smiled warmly when he caught sight of Bo.

'Afternoon! Nice to see someone out here. I was feeling a bit lost and lonesome.' His voice was smooth like thick molasses and he held out his hand to Bo.

'Hello young man. You surprised me.' Bo shook his hand and looked the stranger up and down, wondering where he was coming from.

'Sorry about that, I've been away for a while and I'm trying to find my village.' He sat next to Bo at the base of the tree. 'You look a bit down on your luck,' said the young man.

'So do you,' said Bo. They both laughed and agreed that they'd seen better times. Bo took out his packet of roti and offered to share it. The young man was overjoyed. 'I've not eaten for a couple of days,' he confessed. 'I spent the last of my money catching a ferry over here.'

He tore into the roti like a ravenous dog, barely swallowing with each bite. Bo saw how hungry he was and told him he could finish it. 'Eat up young man. I've got a sweet lady who feeds me every day,' he smiled at the memory and winked mischievously.

'Mmm, my mum makes roti like this. Delicious.' He licked his fingers and thanked Bo before heading on his way. As dusk settled over the island, the young man finally reached his destination, a small wooden house at the edge of the forest. He laughed to himself, imagining his family's surprise when they saw him. I can't wait to see my little sister again.

His steps quickened along the dirt path as he grew nearer to the house. Inside Beatrice was sitting on the verandah, rocking back and forth in her wicker chair. Looking out, she noticed the silhouette of someone familiar strolling up the path. She recognised that light step, almost a dance, as he moved and she knew instantly that it was her brother.

'Paul! Paul! Is that you?' She jumped up out of her seat and screamed out to her parents, happiness nearly stifling her cry. 'Mother, Father! Come quickly. Paul is home.' She rushed down the front steps with her arms outstretched, ready to jump into his but suddenly the figure she saw had stopped moving. He was doubled over, clutching his stomach in pain. 'Paul what's wrong? What's the matter?' Before he hit the floor, Beatrice grabbed his arm and helped him into the house. Their parents joined her, a mixture of happiness and confusion poured out of their mouths, hot and furious, like rainy season showers.

'What's happened? What's wrong? Where have you been? Are you in pain?' They lay him down on the couch and offered him some water to drink. His eyes were bloodshot and his veins, purple and bruised as he clenched his fists. Paul managed to speak a few words, which fell from his lips.

'My stomach is burning. I must have eaten something bad.'

Their mother feared the worst, it was her nature to do so and she questioned him more. 'What have you eaten? Where did you get it?'

He grimaced and stuttered out his reply. 'I ate some roti from a kind old man in the woods.'

Beatrice's skin stung with shame. She could barely speak in reply as she realised she'd poisoned her own brother.

'Which man? What did he look like?' she screamed, shaking him roughly at the shoulders, alarming her parents. But it was too late. Right before their eyes, Paul drew his last breath. His young life drifted out of him, stealing the air from the room and the joy from their hearts.

That was how, on the islands of Trinidad and Tobago, a young girl named Beatrice accidentally murdered her brother.

THE LEGEND OF THE HUMMINGBIRD

Puerto Rico

I'd like to invite you to come way back in time with me. Almost near the beginning of time, when the Taino chief led his people away from the warring Caribs. They settled deep in the El Yunque Mountains of Puerto Rico. Years of fighting had left the mountains weeping with blood from both sides, after violent raids that left the Taino people fleeing into the forest.

Alida was the eldest daughter of the Taino chief. With long black hair and skin the colour of maple leaves, she stood tall with her headdress of feathers, stretching up high like the giant ceiba tree with its canopy of far-reaching limbs.

When the men were out fishing and the women were weaving, she often left the village for some time alone and visited her secret place. It was a vast lagoon of cascading clear water that flowed from the Santo waterfall. On one of these days, Alida hiked through the forest, making sure that no one saw her leave the village.

She climbed down a steep slope of rocks until she reached the foot of the waterfall and dived into the pool. It was blissful, swimming among the fishes, without having to share it with anyone. Afterwards, while drying off on the rocks, she heard a rustling in the trees. Without hesitating, she grabbed her bow and arrow and aimed into the bush.

'Come out. I know you are there,' she called out. She planted her feet firmly on the ground, crouching low like a cat about to pounce. A young man stepped out.

'Who are you and what do you want?' she asked, aiming her arrow directly at his heart.

'My name is Taroo,' he said. But neither one spoke the other's language. She eyed him closely. His tight, black curly hair was covered with a headband of feathers that were different colours from the men in her village.

'I am Alida, eldest daughter of our *cacique*, chief,' she said proudly, lowering her bow. He nodded to show that he understood.

From the amulet of beads tied around his waist she guessed that he belonged to the Caribs, who were at war with her people. She ought to fear him. But he was friendly and beckoned her to stay. Nestled between the roots of a rose apple tree, they shared fruits and coy smiles.

Soon darkness crept in between them and Alida realised she had stayed too long. Her mind raced to thoughts of a trap. Perhaps his people were already raiding her village? She pushed him away, mistrust written all over her face. He shook his head fiercely, 'No. No. I live here alone. I was accidentally left behind,' he tried to assure her.

She returned the next day and was relieved to find him there waiting with small gifts of yellow star fruits and tiny balls of quenépa.

They continued to meet secretly at the flowing waterfall. They swam, picked rose apples and communicated by pointing and sketching in the sand. It was not long before they had fallen in love and were meeting nearly every day.

It was only a matter of time before someone noticed Alida's absence from the village. Her cousin became suspicious about where she was always hurrying off to and he followed her to the waterfall one morning. He stood between the branches of a strangler fig tree, hiding his body between its long, thin limbs. Alida climbed down the rocks towards the lagoon and rushed into the arms of Taroo. Her cousin stared in disbelief, watching them embrace, kiss and explore each other's bodies. Recognising that Taroo was a Carib warrior who would cause them harm, he ran swiftly back to Alida's father to tell him what his daughter was doing.

'She has been secretly meeting with a Carib warrior. Alone! I saw them together.' His words flew through the air like poison arrows, stabbing her father's heart. The chief felt alarmed at what he was hearing. He did not want to believe it. How could his daughter deceive them like this by meeting with an enemy who had raided their villages and tortured their people?

'Is it true that you have been meeting with a Carib warrior?' her father asked.

She lowered her eyes and felt her face burn with shame. This would be considered the ultimate betrayal towards their people. The Caribs had raided their villages many times in the past, torturing the men and capturing the women. He quickly ordered his guards to arm themselves. They planned to go on the attack before they were surprised. They gathered their spears and prepared to hunt Taroo down like a bear, to protect their village. Alida waited in agony until they returned at nightfall and was relieved to see that their hunt had been unsuccessful.

Taroo had slipped away to hide just outside of their village. Once Alida had not shown up to meet him, he suspected that something had happened. Avoiding her father's hunters, he climbed up the slender trunk of a silk cotton tree, where he could be protected by ancestral spirits. From there he kept watch for any sign of his love.

But Alida was now betrothed to another man from the next village. Her father was determined to keep them apart. Overcome with grief, Alida wept at the thought of never seeing Taroo again. The village mothers danced around her, painting her face in bright colours, hanging strings of shells around her neck for the ceremony. They surrounded her with smiles and cheering, believing this to be wonderful news.

'Ah, you look so beautiful,' said one auntie.

'You will be so happy,' said another.

Alida waited until she was alone, and turned in prayer to their god, Yocahu, son of the moon goddess Atabey.

'Take me away from here. I cannot bear it any longer.' She fell to her knees and cried. The god looked down from his place in the sky and took pity upon Alida, soothing her with words of hope.

'Do not be sad Alida, the gods can hear you. I will guide you to freedom and transform you into a beautiful flower.'

As soon as Yocahu uttered those words, Alida vanished into the night. She was changed into a bright red flower and placed safely on the hillside. There she remained, bending towards the sunlight, fluttering softly in the breeze.

But what of Taroo, I hear you ask? He too was overcome with sadness and grief, not knowing what had happened to Alida. He cried out to Yocahu, asking for answers and the god told him of her fate.

'Where can I find her?' replied Taroo, beating the ground with his fist in fury. But it was of no use, she was now one of many red flowers on the hillside and Yocahu did not know which one. To ease Taroo's heartache, the god whispered words of comfort and turned him into a tiny, colourful bird so that he could fly away and find his love Alida.

The next day, two men in the forest marvelled at the sight of a tiny green bird, flitting between the red flowers.

'Look how this bird darts this way and that way so swiftly. Listen to the beating hum of its wings. Let us call it a hummingbird because there is no other sound like it.'

To this day, that is why the colourful hummingbird hovers so closely to the brightest red flowers. It is Taroo, still searching for Alida.

Alma Clarke, Barbados

Nurse

I came here from Barbados when I was 18 years old, in 1960. At the time, my friends and I were in the commercial class at school learning shorthand, typing, booking etc. I had just applied to do nursing at the General Hospital in Barbados when Enoch Powell visited the country. He was the Health Minister in the UK at the time. He came to Barbados to invite us young women in person to come to England to do nursing. I remember him telling us how wonderful it was in Derbyshire. I knew nothing about that part of England but it sounded like an adventure. So I applied to do nursing there, too.

My mum got the letter inviting me to come to England before I was offered a place at the hospital in Barbados. Six weeks after arriving in England, she sent me the letter of invitation that had arrived from the General Hospital in Barbados to become a nurse, but it was too late, I was already here in the UK training to become a nurse in the NHS.

It was the first time that I had travelled out of Barbados before but I never felt nervous. I was happy to get away from my strict Catholic upbringing. This was a wonderful opportunity for freedom. Of course, my mum had given me many words of caution and advice. She told me to 'never kiss a boy' otherwise I'd get pregnant and that only 'loose women' smoked, so I should never smoke. Naturally I believed her and those words remained stuck in my head for quite some time.

I remember travelling through London on the way to Derbyshire. It was autumn at the time and so chilly that you could see smoke coming out of the horses' mouths. I thought 'even the horses smoke over here!' My first impression of London was 'how filthy'. In those days there was a lot of smog from the factories and coal fires. The buildings were black; even Big Ben looked black.

* Please be advised that this account refers to some racially offensive language.

I did my nursing training in Derby with other students. We all shared a place together and I was the only girl from the Caribbean. On my first day, I went into the drawing room where students were relaxing and I saw that everyone was smoking. I was so shocked. My mum's words were ringing in my ears, so I never spoke or mingled with them. I did my work and went straight to my room. I wrote to my mum and told her I wanted to come home because everyone here was loose. Imagine that? Well, I must have looked so miserable that one day Sister Burns called me to her room and asked what was wrong. I started to cry and I confided in her that I was unhappy about being around loose women. She was confused and asked where these women were. After I explained, she put me straight and told me that women who smoked were not depraved. I was puzzled as to why my mum had told me that but looking back I'm sure she was just trying to protect me and prevent me from being led astray.

Not all of her advice was caution, she also taught me good etiquette. I was brought up with impeccable manners, which never left me. Thanks to my chat with Sister, I felt comfortable to speak to the other girls. They were Irish and Catholic like me. I got to know them and they got to know me. I made some really good friends. We all got on very well and went to church together, too. English girls didn't want to do nursing, so Irish and Caribbean girls were invited to come and train.

It was a tough time for black and Irish people back then. We were both discriminated against. I remember seeing signs in the windows: 'No Irish, No Coloureds, No Dogs'.

Colour bars were popular then too in places like youth clubs. But I still socialised with the other nurses and their families. We went to picnics and parties. We had fun and I learnt how to get along with everybody.

In 1964, when the Conservative MP Peter Griffiths got elected in the West Midlands, his campaign slogan was 'If you want a nigger for a neighbour – vote labour'.

Despite all that going on, I was still a feisty young woman. I used to do the bedpan duty at the hospital and one day I went around the ward as usual, calling out 'bedpan!' One of the patients turned to me and said, 'Nurse Clarke, is it true that you people live in trees?' Without skipping a beat I replied, 'Oh yes we do and when Princess Margaret came to Barbados, she slept in the biggest tree, too.'

You can just imagine how that went down! She reported me to the sister of the ward who reported me to the matron, who punished me. I remember it like it was yesterday. Matron sat at her desk, with her back as straight as an iron rod. Her voice was as cold as steel. She said, 'I understand that you insulted royalty?'

I tried to explain what the patient had said to me first but she was not interested in that. She repeated, 'Did you insult royalty or not? I don't want to hear anything else.'

When I said 'yes' she replied, 'Right, for that you won't get ANY break at all today. You will work right through.'

In those days the matron could punish you like that. So I didn't get my break. I worked from 9 a.m. to 9 p.m. without any break at all. There was no justice, but they wouldn't get away with that now. I have spent many years in nursing, in several hospitals across the country.

I'm also an actress and a singer. I wrote a Windrush *poem in 2018 called 'The* Windrush *Generation and the Hostile Environment Bill', which I presented in the Houses of Parliament. It can be found in the Bristol Black Archives. I update it regularly to keep it accurate with the current climate and changes in history. Sadly, many citizens are still suffering under that Bill. It is so important to share our stories so our voices can still be heard.*

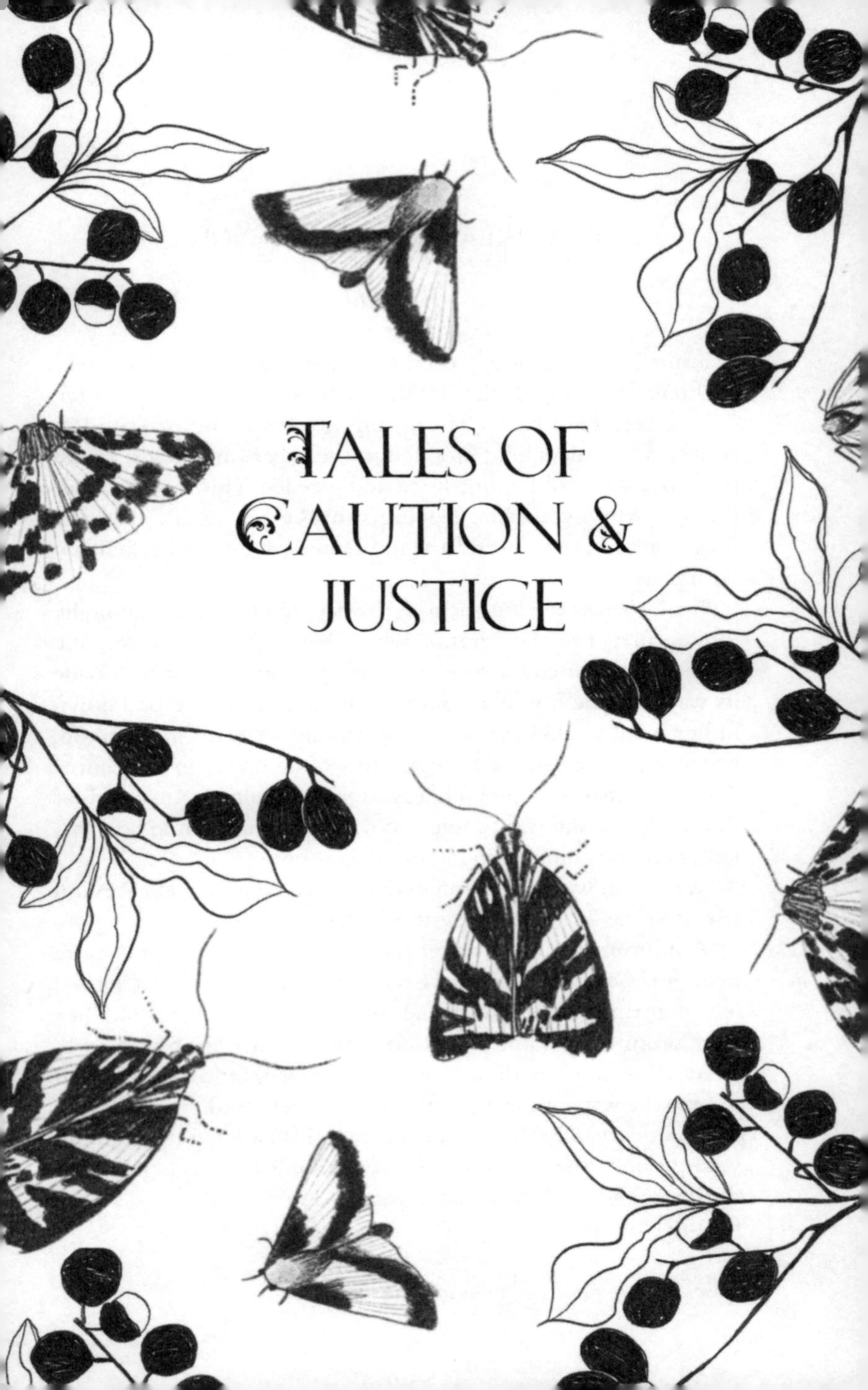
TALES OF
CAUTION &
JUSTICE

You Reap What You Sow

Trinidad

In a small wooden house, on the edge of a forest, lived a family of three. There was Anil, his wife Reshmi and his elderly father. Times were hard back then on this golden island of Trinidad. Anil spent his days bent crooked in the sugar cane fields, where the ground had to be dug, hoed and weeded. This was all under the watchful eye of the blazing sun. Reshmi worked in the sugar mill, sifting and crushing until her dark fingers looked raw with pain.

Finally, when the long arm of the day stretched into the night, they returned to their home, where her work carried on. She picked up the cocoyea broom and swept the dust that had made its way into the home out into the back yard. She settled down in her small kitchen, with its tiny sink underneath the window, heavy-duty oven in the corner, and wooden table in the centre. There she mashed up chickpeas to make dhalpuri roti for their dinner. While she was rolling out the dough, she could hear her father-in-law complaining in the next room.

'When can we eat? I'm hungry? What's taking so long?' Reshmi tried to tune him out, muttering to herself.

'Anil promised me a better life here, a nice house, and more freedom.' Many, like her, had been indentured from India. They'd left their rural villages to sail all the way to the Caribbean. They were promised a home and good food in return for five years of labour. But labour without pay grants you very little freedom. And so here she was, muttering in the kitchen, her words bitter like the bark of the mauby tree with dark thoughts twisting through her young mind. She served out everyone's meal of aloo curry and dhal puri on their kitchen table and tried to make the food stretch for three mouths.

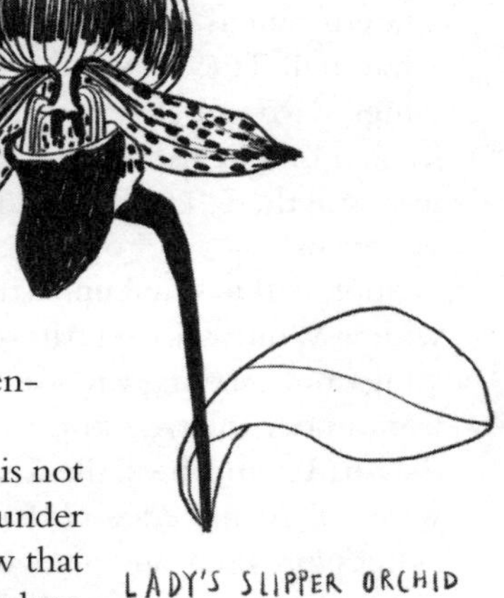

'Is this all there is?' grumbled father-in-law while they ate in silence.

That night, Reshmi approached her husband.

'Can't you put your father somewhere? He's such a burden, another mouth to feed. He complains all night and helps with nothing.' Anil hung his head low, listening in silence.

'He is old Reshmi. Be patient. He is not long for this earth.' His voice cracked under the strain of his own words. He knew that his father was not an easy man to endure, but would probably outlive them both.

Each day brought the same harsh words from his wife, sowing new seeds of doubt in his mind.

'Why can't you leave your father somewhere? Ease our pain just a little?'

Finally, Anil's spirits were worn down. He decided to act. One afternoon, he left the plantation and returned home early to his father. He carefully picked him up out of his chair and carried him into the forest, offering to take him for a walk. Father's frail arms hung loosely around his son's neck. He had not been further than their front yard in such a long time. He breathed in the scent of the white Lady Slipper orchids and went wild when he saw bunches of chenette hanging from the trees. 'Let's stop for a minute, son. Grab me a few chenette to eat.'

CHENETTE TREE

Anil placed his father under the tree and began shelling some of the lime-green fruit. They sat and ate quietly together, sharing a rare moment. They could hear the distant crashing sound of a waterfall. They spotted colourful hummingbirds, beating their wings, darting between the trees and tiny heart-tongued frogs leaping onto leaves. After a while, his father wondered why they were still there. 'Let's go home now, son before the duppies come out for us.'

Soon darkness fell upon them, bringing all the night creatures with it. White-winged bats soared through the sky, flapping their wings and carrying the scent of death. Anil picked his father up from under the tree, but instead of turning back to go the way they had come, he walked towards the deafening sounds of the waterfall. At the edge of the muddy bank, he stood holding his father's frail body and plunged him into the river. The murderous current swept him away. Anil returned home without his father, convincing himself it was for the best.

The years rolled by and Anil and his wife had a son whose life filled them with more joy than they could ever have imagined. Reshmi passed away and left Anil to grow old with his son and

son's wife. She was the new daughter in his life. The woman who fetched and carried and cooked and cleaned. Like his father before him, Anil grew weak and frail, but his mouth was still strong.

'Daughter, I need some cool water to drink.'

'Daughter, I'm too hot here, move me.'

'Daughter, I'm hungry. When will you feed me?'

She sighed heavily as each request piled up high like her basket of washing. She picked up her cocoyea broom, feeling the sharp, prickly edges and wished she could brush the dark thoughts from her mind while sweeping out their rooms. But her face turned sour when food became scarce. Anil's son grew weary in their small wooden hut. His days were filled with back-breaking labour and he saw no end to poverty and hardship.

'Your father is a burden, another mouth to feed. Can't you put him somewhere? Ease our pain just a little?' Her face was twisted and taught, urging him every day. Until one morning, before the sun had risen high in the east, Anil's son picked him up and carried him for a rare walk into the forest. He hung his father's frail arms, loosely around his shoulders. Just as he had done with his own father all those years before. They sat by the river, eating fresh tamarind from the tree, cracking open small pods filled with sweet and sour fruit and chewing the flesh around each seed. It felt so satisfying. Just the two of them. In the distance a tumbling waterfall roared, gushing out cool water to feed the snaking river. Giant moths with dark wings soon fluttered by, signalling the slow end to the day. Before long, daylight disappeared and the night birds began their haunting calls. White-tailed nightjars and great horned owls hooted from their trees, filling the silence with terror. Anil was reminded of this very same moment, all those years before. He looked at his son, who held his head in hands.

'Don't feel bad,' said Anil softly. 'I know that you plan to drown me in the river. I understand why and it is what I deserve. I have loved being your father and wish you a long and happy life.' His eyes filled with tears, soaking the lines on his old face. At that moment, his son felt the true horror of what he was about to do. He shook his head.

'I'm so sorry father. I don't know what I was thinking,' he whispered, hiding his face in shame. He gently picked up his father and carried him home in his arms. When they arrived, his wife was sitting on the verandah, soaking up the night air. She sighed with disappointment at seeing them both return.

He placed his father on the steps and joined his wife, saying, 'My father is the reason I exist and I owe him my life. I cannot take his life from him.' She was stunned by words, but could not disagree and instead of sowing seeds of pain and regret, they found a way to carve out their happiness and reap the rewards of a fruitful life.

The Three Figs

Barbados

There once was a wealthy man named Thomas, who lived in the parish of St Philip on the southern side of the island. His house overlooked the sandy shoreline of Bottom Bay and his land was filled with an abundance of fruit trees, enough to feed the entire village. Golden apples, mangos, tamarind, figs and bright orange ackee trees grew around his home. The air always tasted of sunshine and zest. Yet Thomas was an ill-tempered man who did not notice the beauty in anything around him and focused only on acquiring more wealth.

His neighbour, Jack, owned a small plot of land with only one giant fig tree that stood over 50ft tall. It was the largest fig tree on the island with long, hanging roots that drooped from the branches like a fine, wispy beard, giving it the name 'bearded fig tree'. Jack was a mild-mannered man who was generous to the point that he would give away his last penny, although he rarely had any to give. His fig tree did not often bear fruit but it was so wide that he let villagers gather under its canopy and enjoy the cool shade. Children would swing from its aerial roots, screeching like parrots into the open forest.

'Keep the noise down,' shouted Thomas when he heard the children's voices. 'One of these days I gon' cut down that tree,' he muttered under his breath, fuming on his front ssteps.

One bright, sunny morning, Jack went out into his back yard and noticed a twig from his fig tree with three large figs. They hung like maroon bells just singing to be plucked.

'What an unusual sight, these are the best-looking figs I have seen in a long time,' said Jack, taking them very carefully from the branch. He was so proud of his tree finally bearing fruit that he decided to give them away as they would make a perfect gift. He placed the three figs in a wicker basket and thought to offer them to his neighbour, Thomas. He felt guilty for causing such a disturbance the day before with all the noisy laughter coming from his garden. These ripe figs would be a neighbourly peace offering.

He strolled round to Thomas' house and walked up the white steps, carrying the three figs. Thomas greeted him at the door with a sour-faced scowl.

'My fig tree has finally grown some magnificent fruit, fit for a King!' Jack beamed. Thomas scowled some more.

'I thought I would give them to you as an apology for all the noise the local children made yesterday under my tree. I am sorry we disturbed you.' Jack held up the wicker basket for Thomas to take the figs but he refused.

'What do I need three lousy figs for? I have a gold mine of fruit trees in my own garden. If you think those figs are fit for a King, go and give them to him!' He snapped and shooed Jack off his verandah. Thomas was furious and mostly insulted that his poor neighbour would even consider that his fruit was better than his own. Jack went home and pondered on the idea Thomas had suggested. Why don't I give them to the King? He mused. The figs were swollen and ripe, the largest he'd ever seen, and the King would surely appreciate a gift from their island. He made up his mind that very minute to visit the King and present him with the three figs. Jack kept the figs on their branch and wrapped them in a fresh cloth. The King's palace was in the north of the island in St Peter and he knew it would be a long walk either through the forests or around the island. So he made himself a small supper of cou cou and flying fish to eat on the way if he became hungry.

Jack decided to walk along the sandy coast of crystal white bays. His route along the edge of the island was lined with jagged rocks and dense forests. He held his cloth filled with three figs carefully and set off early the next day. The sea breeze drifted inland, keeping him cool as he stepped lightly through the soft sand. He whistled loudly in reply to the birds, imagining the King's delight at being given three delicious figs. When Jack reached 'The Gap' by Christchurch, his foot suddenly became tangled in a sprawling vine, partially hidden in the sand. He tripped and fell, dropping the cloth holding the three figs.

'Oh no!' Jack cried out loud. 'Trouble don't set up like rain,' he muttered, wishing he had seen that accident coming. He dusted himself off and picked up his parcel. When he opened the cloth, one of the figs had become bruised and no longer looked fit for a

King. He felt so disappointed but decided, 'I might as well eat this one and just give the King two figs.'

In one mouthful he swallowed the slightly squashed fig. It tasted as sweet as sunrise, the best he had ever eaten.

'I must take my time and look out for anything on the ground,' he said to himself and carried on walking briskly but taking care to look where he was placing his feet.

Along the way he clambered over rocks jutting out into the sea, stepped over palm trees leaning across the sand and picked his way through long grass creeping out from the forest. He'd just reached the sparkling blue waters by Alleynes Bay when he heard what sounded like an animal coughing in the trees. He looked around and, seeing no one, just carried on walking. The bark-like cough continued, sounding closer than before. Before he had time to work out what it was, a green monkey jumped out from the trees. Jack saw a flash of golden-green fur rush up to him and grab his small cloth package of figs.

'Stop, you little thief!' he shouted and started to run after the monkey. He was a nimble creature and Jack found himself chasing it into the forest. It scampered up a tree and Jack thought all would be lost but he looked down and saw his bundle of cloth on the ground. The monkey must have become startled and dropped it.

'Ay, just look at my crosses,' moaned Jack wondering why he was having so much trouble with these figs. He picked up the pieces of his gift for the King. He peered inside the cloth and saw that one of the figs had broken off its small branch and was bruised from the fall.

'I might as well eat this bruised one and give the King the last fig, which still looks magnificent,' he thought. Jacked popped the fig into his mouth and savoured the syrupy juice, crunching slowly on the seeds. It was even more delicious than the first fig. He felt sad that he only had one left, but decided that one perfect fig was better than none.

The sun was beginning to dip behind the horizon, leaving a splash of colour across the sky. Holding the last fig close to his chest, Jack hurried on. Once he reached Speightstown, he walked through the streets towards the King's palace, passing kitchen windows and food stalls along the way. The familiar smell of fish cakes, barbecue pig tail and spicy pepper-pot stew floated through the air, making him feel quite hungry. He looked longingly at the last fig but resisted the temptation to eat it. At the palace gates, Jack explained to a guard what he had brought for the King.

'You'll have to wait here at the gate until the King has time to see you,' explained the guard. Jack did not mind and thanked him politely. 'I'll sit under the tree over there until the King is ready,' he replied, pointing to the slender tree with tamarind pods dangling from its branches. He sat down at the tree's roots and leaned back against the trunk, enjoying the chance for a rest. Many hours went by. The palace street lamps lit up the path, finding Jack still waiting under the tree in the evening.

Finally, the guard appeared and announced that the King was ready to see Jack. He accompanied Jack into the palace and explained why he had come. The King was a kind man, known to be thoughtful and patient with his people. He was impressed that Jack had travelled all this way.

'I hear you have a gift for me,' said the King, slightly amused. 'I'm curious to see what you have brought.'

Jack opened his bright cloth and presented the small twig which now only had one fig. 'I'm so sorry my King but I only have one fig to offer you. I started my journey with three figs but on my way, I tripped over and fell. One of the figs was damaged and so I ate it. Later on in my journey I was robbed by a green monkey. A second fig fell onto the ground and was too damaged to give to you and so I ate that one, too.' He hung his head low and offered him the last fig. The King was humbled that Jack should take the trouble to present him with his last fig.

'Thank you for being so honest,' said the King. 'You could have lied and made up any excuse for the missing figs. I will try your gift.' He took the last fig from Jack and swallowed it whole. His face lit up with joy as he tasted the fresh sweetness. The King nodded his head in agreement. 'Ah, it is the taste of golden sun rays! Indeed this is the most exquisite fig I have ever eaten. Tell me about your fig trees. I want to know more.'

The King listened as Jack spoke of his single fig tree, the largest on the island. He told the King of all the families who came to picnic under the tree's canopy of wide branches and of the children who swung from the aerial roots. He explained how rarely the tree bore fruit. The King was even more touched by Jack's kindness and offered him a reward.

'For your generosity, honesty and sincerity, I will fill your cloth with gold goins.' The King signalled to his guard and a bag of gold coins were placed into his cloth. Jack was overwhelmed with gratitude. He had not been seeking for any kind of reward. He bowed graciously to the King and made his journey back home, skipping most of the way.

When Jack's neighbour, Thomas, heard of his new-found riches he was overcome with envy. 'If that foolish Jack can receive such a fine sum from the King, I can definitely do much better,' he raged and plotted to find a way to outdo Jack. He cut down all the fresh figs from his trees in his garden and piled them up in his lorry to take to the King. 'Wait until the King sees my magnificent figs. He will surely repay me with a lorry filled with gold coins!'

Thomas set off for the palace imagining what he would do with all his wealth. 'I can build an extension to my home. I can buy Jack's plot of land and own the entire area. Maybe I can buy all the land in the village!'

It took Thomas less than half an hour to drive from his home in the south to the King's palace in the north. When he arrived, the guard explained that he would have to wait as the King was busy. This did not sit well with Thomas. He was too eager to get his hands on the gold coins.

'I am a busy man too and the King will want to hear from me. Tell him at once that I am here!' He raised his voice and continued to argue with the guard, who refused to disturb the King. Thomas' loud voice, screeched through the open windows, past the portraits hanging on the walls and right into the throne room, where the King was holding council.

'What is all of the commotion?' He asked his advisors, who were with him. Everyone shook their heads and shrugged their shoulders. Seeing as no one knew, the King himself marched outside to his courtyard to see what was wrong. He found Thomas standing at the gates in a heated debate with one of his guards.

'I'm sorry my King, but this man refuses to wait peacefully until you are ready,' the guard tried to explain but Thomas butted in and started to speak over him. 'Your guard is so ignorant. All muscle and no mind! He was too stupid to listen to me. I was trying to tell him that I have bought you a mountain of precious figs from my very own garden, my King.'

Thomas's chest swelled with pride and he continued to speak, filling the King's ears with his boasting and bravado. The King was initially perplexed, wondering why this man would unexpectedly bring him all of these figs. He watched Thomas' mouth moving incessantly, braying like a horse, and he soon remembered the humble Jack, who was patient and gracious. The King saw through Thomas's insincere actions, realising at once that he had come hoping to be rewarded with gold for his figs.

'Man have cow and he still look for milk!' the King bellowed. He turned to his guards and ordered them to remove him from the palace grounds immediately. Thomas was horrified. He quickly turned and fled as the guards began pelting his own figs at him from his lorry. He dashed into the hills, running as if nine devils were chasing him and didn't arrive back home until later that evening.

Word soon spread around the island of how Thomas went to the King for gold but came back empty-handed with his tail between his legs. Jack enjoyed his new-found wealth and still let villagers picnic under his giant fig tree. When you visit Barbados today, you can see these wonderful trees dotted around the island, with their long aerial roots hanging like wispy beards. These are the bearded fig trees after which the island is named: *Los barbados*, the bearded ones.

No Justice for the Devil

Suriname

One day, the Devil and God were having a chat. They often got together on mutual ground, somewhere in between heaven and earth. It was always an opportunity for them to reflect, share news and occasionally compete with each other for our attention. Time ceased to exist for them. They could pause, go back or forward whenever they wanted. They could see every possible outcome to every situation, depending on how they looked at it.

On this particular day, the world was in chaos from Devil's point of view. Fires were spreading, mountains were melting, animals were disappearing and people were frantic and miserable. Greed and insecurity had joined forces, like an unrelenting hurricane. They came twisting, hurtling and smashing through the world and settled down comfortably together in many people's hearts. Which left very little space for anything else.

The world was just where it needed to be, from God's point of view. It was bubbling over like a pressure cooker with everyone's desires waiting to burst forth. Out of the chaos would come calm and the seeds of kindness had been scattered everywhere, ready to thrive and flourish from the carnage.

'You always look at the bad side of things,' mused God, sprinkling them both in rays of laughter.

'That's not true,' snapped Devil, with a furrowed brow. 'I always get blamed for anything bad. There's no justice for me, no matter what I do.'

God sighed, 'What makes you think that?'

Devil thought for a moment, sending waves of heat out into the atmosphere. 'Let's do an experiment. I'll prove to you that my reputation precedes me, even if I do good.'

God was intrigued. With endless possibilities available, it would be wonderful to be surprised. Devil asked God to create a large rock and place it on a path, anywhere on earth. So God forged a piece of granite. Irregular in shape, with flecks of glassy quartz, feldspar and shiny black mica. It was placed in the middle of a dusty path, just outside of Djumu village in Suriname. The rock was small enough to step over but large enough to sit on. Devil conjured up a small sack of gold, which was placed at the side of the rock.

'Now wait and see what happens,' said Devil with great satisfaction.

It was an exceptionally bright day, with an intoxicating array of scents bursting from the rainforest alongside the path. Towering cannonball trees with round balls of fruit mingled with pink and white lotus flowers, overflowing onto the path. A young man named Joe soon came strolling along. He was heading into the village, whistling as he made his way. His thoughts were elsewhere and he didn't notice the rock, lying in the middle of the path.

'OUCH,' he cried, stumbling into it and hitting his toes. 'What devil left that there?' He bent down to rub the pain away from his foot, not noticing the bag of gold, and then carried on his way into the village.

Devil turned to God, 'You see how I got blamed for that accident?'

God shrugged and waited to see what would happen next. After a little while, Mrs D'souza, an elderly woman, came along. She was enjoying listening to the bird calls echoing from the forest when she spotted an agouti darting into the bushes. She too didn't notice the rock lying in the middle of the path.

'OWWW' she cried, stumbling into it, hitting her toes. 'What the hell was that?' She checked to see if her foot was OK, not seeing the bag of gold next to the rock, and then carried on her way into the village.

Devil and God both raised their eyebrows in wonder. Things were starting to play out just as Devil had expected. After a while, two young girls came along. They'd been swimming in the river and were making their way home. As they approached the rock, one of the girls, named Nella, noticed the bag. 'I wonder what's this?' she said and picked it up to show her friend. They opened it together and peered inside, seeing that it was filled with gold coins. 'Praise be to God! What a heavenly surprise!' they both exclaimed, jumping up on the spot and hugging each other. They swiftly made their way home, shouting, 'Thank you God, thank you!'

Devil turned to God triumphantly, 'You see? What did I tell you? There's no justice for me, no matter what I do.'

Mary Seacole

Whenever you unravel a time in history and journey across the length and breadth of oceans and borders, you are sure to find stories filled with wars. Fierce battles are fought, people and countries are traded. In the midst of those tales, there is often someone who refuses to be defined or constrained by the outcome of those wars. Someone who stirs up the pot, bringing all of their knowledge and fervour with them. One such person was Mary Seacole. She was a traveller, an entrepreneur and a nurse who is often remembered as a hero for risking her life to save others and daring to go where many would not.

Like a rich medley of Caribbean gumbo influenced by Creole, African and British flavours, Mary brought a mixture of cultures, knowledge and strength to everything that she did. Born Mary Jane Grant, she grew up with her brother and sister on the verdant island of Jamaica, with its towering Blue and John Crow mountains, filled with rainforests abundant with tropical grass and healing herbs. She was the daughter of a Creole woman and a Scottish soldier. Born in a time when ships brought enslaved Akan people from Fort Kormantin, in Ghana, to Jamaica. They were forced to work the Caribbean land for sugar cane, needed to sweeten the British cakes and tea. Many soldiers were stationed on the island guarding the jewels of sugar, coffee and rum. Regiments were filled with British soldiers, Creoles and African men who were eventually set free after their service.

On one searing hot day in her childhood, Mary sat playing on the steps of the long veranda of their boarding house, Blundell Hall. A scorpion crawled past, hoping to find a crack to disappear into. Sunshine bleached every corner of the buildings, but the verandah offered shade from the guinep trees for her toys to rest in. Lined against the brick wall were her dolls, wrapped in bandages and leaves. Each doll lay on its side, unwell with a fever or stomach bug. She'd seen her mother do this many times with real people, sick army officers who stayed at their hall. Mary tended to her dolls, whispering words of comfort, when her mother's voice called out of an open window, halting the imaginary play.

'Mary! Mary! Where are you child? Fetch me some more bissy from the tree.' Her voice was sharp and insistent, echoing around the courtyard. It was not something you ignored. Perhaps one of their guests was wounded? Mary thought, racing to her mother's side.

'Something bit this soldier badly and the poison is working its way through,' her mother explained, patting his forehead with a wet cloth. Mary looked on as a young man lay under a mosquito net, twisting and squirming in bed. His whole body was shivering, even his teeth were chattering while beads of hot sweat poured down his forehead. His lips were no longer pink, but a dull, lifeless blue. An angry, blistering rash creeped along his arm, bringing prickly pangs of pain with it.

Mary noted all of the symptoms and knew what to do. She was often sent to fetch, boil or pound herbs. Each day, her mother passed on the knowledge of how to use African remedies and island herbs to heal and cure the sick soldiers in their care.

Mary ran out of the room, hurried across the courtyard and past an open corridor of rooms at the back, where their land was a fragrant paradise, bursting with colour. Golden oranges, sour grapefruits, lemons and limes hung from the trees like jewels waiting to be picked. The smell of fresh ginger and dandelion filled the air. She stepped carefully, avoiding the sharp green nettles and writhing snakes, looking for what her mother needed.

Mary could recite the names of flowering plants and trees, knowing exactly what should be used when someone was suffering:

Fever grass, leaf of life,
Bitter cerasee.
Soursop, spirit weed,
Leaves of comfrey.

She collected some herbs and dashed back to help her mother. Mary was always overjoyed when a fever was brought low, wounds were healed and poor stomachs were made mighty again. These soldiers were not just patients to her but friends who she saw come and go with the tide that sailed from England.

Early one morning, before sunrise stretched across the sky, Mary followed the gentle smell of sea breeze and made her way to the harbour. She stood at the edge of the island ankle deep in sand, watching the ships disappear across the horizon leaving a deep longing in her heart. Like a red-billed hummingbird darting across the skies, she longed to travel and explore the world.

'One day that will be me, sailing all the way to England,' she decided, breathing in the salty sea air. She imagined boarding one of those ships named after ancient Greek gods and heroes. Diana, Achilles, Orestes. At times, she gazed at maps, tracing her fingers along the route to England.

It was perhaps of no surprise that her dream came true. As a young woman, Mary made her first trip to England to visit her father's family. She sailed out across the turquoise waters of the

Caribbean sea, leaving behind the poinsettia trees, tumbling waterfalls and an island already filled with over 300,000 black slaves.

At times, she noticed frosty stares from English people whose demeanour matched their bleak weather. She was a quiet young girl, and used to seeing white people but they were not all used to seeing Mary with her cinnamon brown complexion. The English street boys, never tired of stopping suddenly in the street, mouth open, pointing at Mary and her black friend.

'I am a Creole with Scottish blood in my veins,' Mary thought, puzzled at this behaviour. The boys stared and brought attention to the colour of their skin. How dark it was. How different. How strange.

'I am only a little brown – a few shades duskier than the brunettes whom you all admire so much.'

Mary did not let their behaviour concern her. She offered a broad smile, maintaining her cheerful disposition. She had other things on her mind. For now, she had tasted the sweet freedom of travel and wanted so much more. After that first visit, she returned to England again, carrying preserves and pickles from Jamaica to sell. It was an excellent way to fund her travels. She was an independent, free woman yearning to see the rest of the world, its people and culture. Like the long-tailed Bahama mockingbird with its persistent song, more island countries called out to her waiting to be explored.

With an enterprising spirit, Mary sailed to Cuba, Haiti, the Bahamas and Panama in central America, bringing back unique items to sell and trade in Jamaica to finance her trips. She soaked up each island's treatments and cures for tropical diseases, amassing more nursing knowledge.

Finding ways to help others in need was always uppermost in her mind. One morning in 1854, back in her hometown of Kingston, Mary made her way to the entrance of Blundell Hall. Her mother and husband, Edwin Seacole, had both passed away, leaving her to run the boarding house alone. She sat on the veranda, cordially greeting any guests who passed by. Her hair was pinned back, with tight cascading waves and small pearl earrings, dangling on either side. Her long wide dress fanned out like an umbrella, adding to her graceful presence. She picked up the newspaper and gasped in horror. The headlines leaped out from the front page:

> War in the Crimea between Russia and Turkey

A battle was taking place, far away across the Atlantic Ocean. Russia was at war with Turkey over who controlled the Danube. Britain and France had joined the war, trying to help Turkey defeat the Russians. Mary's eyes scanned across the page, fear creeping into her heart with each word that she read:

> Hospitals are overflowing, without enough space to treat all the patients. More soldiers are dying from tropical diseases than gunfire.

Mary was concerned for her friends. 'Many of my British sons who I have fed and nursed at my house, are fighting in this war. I must find a way to go and help them,' she decided and packed immediately to sail for England. 'My skills as a doctress nursing soldiers through cholera and yellow fever outbreaks would surely be in great demand,' she thought, packing as many natural remedies as she could. Little did Mary know what an insurmountable mountain she would need to climb, filled with rejection and disappointments, in order to become a nurse in the Crimean War.

Armed with favourable testimonials including one from a former medical officer, Mary made countless applications to the War Office for the role of hospital nurse. Her tenacious spirit saw her pen letter after letter, remaining hopeful for an interview with the Secretary of War. But each application was greeted with silence. Undaunted by this initial rejection, Mary applied to the Medical Department.

Like an elegant potoo bird, with its mixture of brown and black wings resembling the bark of a tree, Mary perched wide eyed. She sat watching and waiting outside the Medical

Department quarters for endless hours but no one would see her, a woman travelling alone expecting to go to war. By the end of the day, her heart slowly sank to her knees. She felt helpless. If this was Jamaica or any other Caribbean island, they would have known her worth, valued her knowledge of how to treat the ailments these soldiers were suffering from.

Cholera, diarrhoea, bullet and knife wounds. Didn't they realise that sometimes the simplest remedies were the best? She knew and recited them like a familiar friend:

Mustard seeds for aches and pains
Cinnamon bark in tea
Calomel powder for yellow fever
Aloe and soursop leaves.

A bright new day brought with it new ideas and opportunities, filling Mary with renewed vigour. She heard that Florence Nightingale was already in Crimea and more nurses were being sent. Another plan formed in Mary's mind, this time to travel with these British nurses. So she sent an application, feeling quite sure that they would be glad of her services. Determined to increase her chances of enrolment, Marry obtained the address of the Secretary of War and perched once again, bright eyed and expectant, on a seat in his great hall. She waited all morning and all afternoon to be seen. She sat mute and motionless, watched by the eyes staring down from paintings on the stone walls. The minutes and hours crept past, like a thief stealing the day.

Shuffle, shuffle, click, click, step. The noble staff bustled past, completely ignoring Mary, their faces filled with loathing at the brown-skinned woman still sitting in their grand hall. Day after day, she returned, sitting silently in a corner, hoping to be seen. The resentful looks and tuts fell from everyone's lips who walked past. Over time, the air filled with bitterness, which chipped away at Mary's resolve, leaving painful wounds in its place. 'Is she still here? What does she think she's doing?' came the voices echoing down the hall.

In that moment, Mary finally gave up, knowing that she was beaten and would not be permitted to speak with the Secretary of War. She left with her head held high and within days a new opportunity presented itself in the form of an interview with one of Florence Nightingale's companions.

Mary dusted off her rejections and talked enthusiastically of her experience in medicine. The lady examined Mary's broad face, listening without any expression, before promptly dismissing her.

'All of the nursing roles have been filled, Mrs Grant,' came the curt reply. Her steely eyes bore sharply into Mary. They seemed to say, 'And we would not give you a role even if there was a vacancy.'

That night, a foul stench continued to drift through the streets of London. It rose from decaying sewers and rotting fluids. It passed by the slaughterhouses and cow sheds that lined the streets. It gathered strength from the smell of grease-boiling dens in the air. It crept into people's hearts and minds, mixing with shadowy, dark thoughts. Thoughts that entered Mary's mind. She stood on the cobbled streets and breathed in the filthy night air, sobbing quietly to herself.

'Are people here filled with so much prejudice against my skin colour that they would not accept my selfless motives? Is my blood different from theirs, just because it flows beneath a darker shade of skin?'

She cried long, angry tears, ignoring any passers-by who cast quizzical looks as they hurried home in the dark mist. She cried for all the hours she had spent explaining her medical experience to anyone in a position of power. She cried for the futility of racial prejudice that may have prevented her from being accepted as a nurse and she cried for the soldiers whom she knew would benefit from her help.

As we all know, the dark shadows of night melt away when daylight tiptoes in. Mary woke up the next morning feeling renewed vigour for her plans. Like a great spotted woodpecker that is not afraid to be seen or heard, using its powerful beak to hammer holes in tough trees, Mary found strength in her own resourcefulness.

'I can fund a ship and carry my own supplies. I will open a hotel to treat the sick soldiers by myself,' she declared, determined that it would be a success. She called on her friends of doctors and generals who knew of her work in Jamaica, asking them to donate and assist however they could. And on 25 January 1855, Mary sailed over 3,000 miles with her business friend, Thomas Day, from London to Crimea.

She had no fear of setting up a new establishment, after managing her previous businesses and helping to run her brother's hotel in Panama. Surely this venture would be as welcome as the sea breeze? Plans were made and a site selected on Spring Hill. It was a stone's throw away from where the soldiers were stationed in Balaclava, making it easy for them to stay or send messengers to collect home comforts. Mary called it 'The British Hotel'. To some, it may have looked like simple huts with tin roofs but to Mary and the soldiers it was a suite of buildings. An acre of muddy land was home to an iron storehouse packed with shelves filled with provisions, sleeping rooms, a canteen for dining, stables for officers' horses and mules, sties squawking with livestock of fowls and geese, and wooden outhouses for staff quarters. The harsh winds blew in from the sea, turning the air to brittle frost, but the soldiers found warmth inside the British Hotel, with a cheerful welcome from a coal fire and hearty meals made by Mary's cooks.

'Thank you for your kindness Mother Seacole and indeed for your delicious pork,' a weary soldier smiled and licked his lips after dinner, offering words of praise. Mary's heart soared, knowing that she had done the right thing by coming. She loved nothing more than to make everyone feel comfortable, well fed and their ailments treated with care.

Just across the way in Scutari, Florence Nightingale was tending to soldiers in her hospital. She walked through the quiet wards at night, drifting silently with her lamp, between the groups of soldiers reading or sleeping. Nurses and orderlies shuffled quietly by, speaking in hushed tones. They wore the pained expressions of those who have seen far too much trauma.

Mary split her time between running the hotel and tending to the soldiers on the battlefield. Each day she rose at 4 a.m. to pluck poultry, prepare meals and mix medicines. By 7 a.m. coffee was prepared and served to those in need before breakfast. She would visit the Balaclava hospital across from her hotel and take books and papers for the sick soldiers. Sometimes she mounted her horse, loaded it up with supplies and galloped near the front lines. Gunpowder clouded the air, often making it difficult for anyone to see. Bleeding, thirsty and exhausted, soldiers looked out through the mist and felt relief at the familiar sight of her bright red scarf.

'It's Mother Seacole! Look here she comes!' cried one young man, shivering in a ditch. He clutched his gun as best he could with aching, frostbitten fingers. The air was heavy with the miseries of winter and the sound of gunfire roaring all around. Mary headed in their direction, carrying refreshments and bandages in her large bag, oblivious to being under fire. In the distance a loud explosion pierced the air. The deafening sound grew closer, becoming more insistent.

'Mother LIE DOWN', a voice screamed across the field, as a large cannon ball came flying in Mary's direction. She dropped her bag and threw herself face down into the mud, as the cannon whizzed past, narrowly missing her head. The young soldier had saved her life, for which she was eternally grateful.

Once the war had ended, Mary returned penniless to England. All of her wealth had been drained in Crimea. Always brimming with ideas, she turned to writing and published her autobiography in 1857. Her book, *The Wonderful Adventures of Mrs Seacole in Many Lands*, was filled with details of her travels and the Crimean War, and it was indeed a success.

She lived out the rest of her summer days in England, and when the harsh winter months set in she stayed in Jamaica, enjoying the caress of the sea breeze and the familiar sounds from the rainforest, until her death on 14 May 1881.

The memory of her remarkable deeds and tenacious spirit remain indelibly stamped in the heart of both islands. If you visit a ward in Kingston Hospital, you'll find Mary Seacole House. When you step into the National Portrait Gallery in London, Mary's portrait is displayed proudly. In front of St Thomas' Hospital, just across from the River Thames, near Big Ben, you can see an elegant 10ft bronze statue of Mary Seacole, the Jamaican nurse and entrepreneur who served the British soldiers during the Crimean War.

BIBLIOGRAPHY

Some of the stories in this collection have been passed down to me by my mother and grandmother during my childhood. A few stories were shared with me by renowned storytellers Grace Hallworth, Baden Prince and Winston Nzinga. Other tales I used as reference and inspiration when delving into my own archive of books and those from libraries listed below.

Bennett, Louise, *Anancy and Miss Lou* (Kingston, Jamaica: Sangster's Book Stores, 1979).

Charles, Faustin, *Under the Storyteller's Spell* (London: Puffin, 1991).

Grant, Rosamund, *Caribbean and African Cookery* (London: Grub Street Publishing, 2003).

Hearn, Lafcadio, *Two Years in the French West Indies* (1890).

Mahabir, Kumar, et al., *Caribbean Indian Folktales* (San Juan, Trinidad and Tobago: Chakra Publishing House, 2005).

Sánchez González, Lisa, *The Stories I Read to the Children: The life and writing of Pura Belpré, the legendary storyteller, children's author, and New York public librarian* (Centro Press, 2013).

Seacole, Mary, *The Wonderful Adventures of Mrs Seacole in Many Lands* (1857).

The American Folklore Journal.